S0-BCR-883

The Skein

A Story Of Secrets

Elizabeth Schaeffer

WILSONVILLE PUBLIC LIBRARY

To Nika Corales, for her continuing guidance, patience, and support.

Order this book online at www.trafford.com
or email orders@trafford.com

Most Trafford titles are also available at major online book retailers.

© Copyright 2012 Elizabeth Schaeffer.
Cover Photo by Astrida Schaeffer
All rights reserved. No part of this publication may be reproduced, stored in a retrieval
system, or transmitted, in any form or by any means, electronic, mechanical, photocopying,
recording, or otherwise, without the written prior permission of the author.

Printed in the United States of America.

ISBN: 978-1-4669-3310-1 (sc)
ISBN: 978-1-4669-3311-8 (hc)
ISBN: 978-1-4669-3312-5 (e)

Library of Congress Control Number: 2012908224

Trafford rev. 05/10/2012

 www.trafford.com

North America & international
toll-free: 1 888 232 4444 (USA & Canada)
phone: 250 383 6864 ♦ fax: 812 355 4082

WILSON THE PUBLIC LIBRARY

Contents

To Stephen

With love for all his help and for just being Stephen.

MAJOR CHARACTERS:

Annie Westwood / Lady Anne Riddecoombe / Ann

Braithwaite (butler)

Sir Arthur Riddecoombe

Allen Herrick

Mrs. Dorothy Dray

Vicar and Amity Matthews

Percival Riddecoombe

Percival Riddecoombe (again)

Letty Hampton-Gray

Superintendent Robert Oakes of Scotland Yard

Gil Harkness

Colonel Lord Farthington

Lady Felicity Farthington

Major Alex Atherton

Miss Makepeace

Major General Grayson Hoving

Dr. Coates

Charles Herrick

Chapter 1

Unsettled Weather

E ngland—spring 1949. The land here in the West Country, even after the long years of war, shows no scars, reveals no secrets. The scars and the secrets are hidden in the minds of the survivors. Sorrow in the minds of many. Anger in the minds of many. Guilt in the minds of many. In the minds of a very few, there was a shadowy empty space where guilt could reasonably have been found, and was not. Those minds still wove a skein—a dangerous skein—of intrigue and deceit, here where the scars and secrets of war were real, but could not be seen.

This is the story of a few brave but unlikely friends who uncovered those secrets and those scars by following their shadowy strands into the intricate heart of the skein.

In late May in this West Country, the fields were all the many greens of newness. Tall trees, notable for their great age, were incongruously unfurling brilliant green leaves radiant in their new beginnings. In the rose garden of High Place Old Lodge, no blooms yet added scarlet or vibrant cerise to the lush green, but there was a brilliant rose-red in the lovely dress of Lady Riddecoombe, glowing in the center of the lush green so that she seemed to be the one rose—the one perfect rose in the garden.

"Damnation all to hell and back!" Lady Riddecoombe was not pleased. Nor, from her words, was she entirely British. She was certainly not the aristocratic British rose to be expected in this, the essence of an aristocratic English garden. Yet she spoke with a quiet tone and an undeniably refined accent at uncomfortable odds with the words she spoke. She was seated on a white Victorian garden bench, uncomfortable as only the Victorians could make them, surrounded by her own personal correspondence on her own personal stationery.

The stationery was a light blue gray with a white deckled border, and obviously not a personal choice. She had been given the choice of colors and styles—of course she had. However, since she had been the young bride of the wealthy Sir Arthur Riddecoombe, what choice had she but light Wedgwood blue with white deckled edges? Was that not what was to be expected? The new Lady Riddecoombe had learned very quickly that the expected was, well, to be expected. One judged a new Lady Riddecoombe by a certain standard. It was always the standard of those who expected the best—the standard of Sir Arthur Riddecoombe, to give an example. For him, the best was always to be expected. The best, to give an example, in the subtle art of blackmail, which he had refined and polished so assiduously in such a perfection of secrecy. The very best in the sophisticated, Janus-faced, art of humiliation. He took pride in perfecting his art. He had begun in childhood and, by this time, had reached a very high level indeed.

Anne, on the other hand, was a mere beginner. In a game in which she had no experience nor, to her credit, any natural aptitude, she learned slowly. She had not always been Lady Riddecoombe. She had been young, of course, awkward, over-tall, red-haired Annie Westwood as she grew up, the only child of an upper-class younger son of a younger son in a fashionable but not impressive area of West London. Her parents were scholarly rather than aristocratic—born in the higher classes, but not of them. Her father even taught school. Granted, at a well-respected public school, but still, not the accepted thing, not at all. Her genteelly timid mother had stood firm for once and insisted that Annie be sent to the States with many other children at the beginning of the war, rather against the wishes of her father who considered it "unBritish." Her mother had been right. The London house had become a smoking crater halfway through the Blitz. Her parents, thankfully, had been staying at their small summer place, a made-over tenant farmer's cottage really, a very small house on a rather large acreage in Wiltshire. It was all they had left. It was part of the land of the West Country.

Annie, one of the many British children sent to the States for safety during the war, spent those years on a thriving farm in Kansas. She was conscious of a great deal of conflict within her growing sense of herself. She felt that she had, in her father's words, "let the side down." Yet she was supremely happy there while her home and former life were being destroyed. The family to which she temporarily belonged had requested her partly because her foster mother had a family of three strong, healthy boys and was rather afraid of trying again and making it four. Her foster mother loved her dearly, and a bond formed that sent the affection back and forth between them in easy comfort. It was here Ann learned what it felt like to be loved. It would be a long time before she felt that again. The three boys had seen her as a means of allowing them to have teams of two against two of whatever sport was in season. Summer meant baseball on the dusty diamond by the small schoolhouse. Fall meant a rather abrupt introduction to football, tag football, their mother insisted, but the term had been vaguely defined. The boys had called it rag football, which was more appropriate, somehow. Winter meant basketball in the school gym.

Ann and the boys reached the gym by plowing through knee-deep snow against a high wind that always came at them from whichever direction they were trying to go. Ann developed a joy and a skill in basketball. Annie, now Ann, developed a set of skills Annie never would have dreamed of. She now had skills she was proud of, but skills she did not write home to mother about. London, even fashionable

West End London, did not allow for robust growth in its young. Skills like tramping through knee-deep snow to school and possibly even deeper snow on the way home were not needed in the gritty, grimy slush of London. Skills like skipping stones on the cow pond were not part of a young London lady's upbringing. Her real love and her real skill was writing.

Later, as Lady Riddecoombe, she remembered the yellow, green-lined Goldenrod pads of school paper with great fondness. She was good at writing, and with her different perspective, keen observation and deep understanding of human nature, she was able to write about things around her in ways that made her classmates see them in a new light and appreciate this newcomer from across the pond. She sharpened her perceptions on everything around her: trees in winter, clouds and their indications of the coming weather, her friends, and, on another sheet not to be shown to anyone, her enemies. She had few enemies and many friends. English teachers loved her. Math teachers tolerated her, barely. She was happy.

Then the war came to an end, or rather the fighting came to an end. For some, the struggle continued. Certainly the blackmail continued. The misdirection of arms, art, and other things of beauty continued. Arthur was happily busy at the things he did best.

Chapter 2

A V-Shaped Depression

Then came the victory—the welcome home that should have been so joyous.

Welcome home to a hole in the London mud where her home should have been and to two exhausted and feeble parents, aged well beyond their years, who now lived on their huge acres in their tiny summer home. The house had originally been a tenant farmer's cottage, It was now old, cramped, and damp. Ann's room was taken by the nurse her parents relied upon. There was no room for Annie in the house or in the lives of these two gray people depleted of all the colors of life. These two strangers were desperate to take care of "the problem of Annie" before the death they could already feel so near.

Her parents lived long enough to reintroduce her to her neighbors at High Yews. Sir Fredrick Riddecoombe had lost his money to gambling and their home, High Place, with the war. It still stood at the top of the hill but was no longer theirs. The Allies had arrived. They bought and they held.

When the eldest Riddecoombe son, Arthur, safely home from a financially successful war, had tried to buy the estate back, all he could buy—argue he never so winningly, offer he never so much—was the Dower House, which he promptly bought and renamed High Place Old Lodge, far more fitting for a bachelor. It came with only a minute, a shamefully minute, strip of land adjoining the Woodhouse acres. He was furious. He was brought into this world to have what he wanted to have no matter how he got it. He was a highly successful military man who had control of the flow of arms and equipment over a significant part of the Western Front. How ironic that he could not return successfully to his own family seat, to the land that was rightfully his! All right, there were other ways. If he couldn't buy the house, at least he could marry the land. The land belonged to Annie's parents. It was all they had left. It solved the problem of Annie.

So here was Annie, now also without a home. She was not really a lady at all. She could shoot baskets, but not grouse. She had no social skills. She had developed a stride intended to cover the long spaces of the Midwest, but had definitely not acquired a graceful way with staircases. Further, she came with red,not auburn but red, hair. Sir Arthur's crowning blow was that this scarecrow of a wife, who granted him his dream of the Woodhouse acres, stood a good three to four inches over Sir Arthur's slightly balding head.

It was Sir Arthur now, with her parents' impending demise, who would own the Woodhouse acres next to, marching with, the pathetic little strip of the Riddecoombe property that was still his.

Annie's parents lived barely long enough to be present at the wedding. They had solved the problem of Annie. They died content.

Chapter 3

A Title For A Title

Arthur's friends joked that the marriage had been a mere transfer of titles. Anne, now with an *e*, acquired the title to her name, and Arthur acquired the title to her land. His friends considered it elegant in its simplicity.

It was much more than that. Much more. Annie/Ann/Anne knew nothing for certain anymore—not even her own name. Anne had simply been considered more befitting a lady, and so she became Lady Anne Riddecoombe. She could see it on her stationery. Lady Anne Riddecoombe. She was as much his property as her land had become.

She knew how to be Annie and knew she had never liked it. She knew she had loved being just Ann. The same man who had added the *Lady* had added the *e*. She was helpless to change either one, and he knew it. Further, he knew she didn't like it. He liked that too. He waited until all his friends had seen her as a redhead, although the veil had softened that at the wedding, and then he chose the tint on the chart that had changed it to a soft rich auburn. Then he was able to stand to one side and watch his friends appreciate the difference, The fact that the auburn was much more flattering and that she liked the look of it only made things more confusing. He saw that she was taller than he. He let her know, so kindly and with such loving teasing, that this was not acceptable. She began to slouch and wear flat-heeled shoes. Anger and frustration can make even the most attractive face unappealing. That delighted him. Then he took her to the most exclusive dress shops and had clothes made for her without the slouch. It would never do to slouch before the couturier. Then, of course, when the Riddecoombes had guests, he would insist that she wear her most stunning dresses—the ones that the two lovebirds had decided upon. Of course, the gorgeous frocks would look hideous on her. Rather, more to the point for Sir Arthur, she would look hideous in them. Nothing wrong with the frocks, absolutely nothing wrong with them. So he would smile proudly at her, and his friends would snicker and cough behind their hands. Worst of all, she would blush. A redhead is never at her best blushing. He knew that too. He knew so much. So very much.

That kind of knowing had been based on long practice. She realized that. He had always been short for his age. She remembered him from those few summer vacation times when they were in groups of children always arranged by age. Of course, Napoleon's name came into the conversation as soon as the other boys learned who Napoleon had been. She remembered the merciless teasing he received. What she could not know was how he got his revenge.

Small children can hide more easily than tall ones. They can learn to be very quiet. Like little mice, they can be quiet. Then they can overhear things. Little pitchers can have big ears. Big ears combined with retentive memories can be dangerous when they are as highly motivated by revenge as those of little Arthur. Revenge taught memories to sort these things heard and to retain the most useful of them. The most useful things, Arthur soon found out, were things that could be used against the speaker. Used first for a bigger share of someone else's candy. Then all of someone else's candy. Then the laugh would be on the one suddenly without candy. The candyless one did not dare defend himself without letting out the secret that had been so safe. Until now. Until Arthur.

What had proved to work in school could work in many other more complex situations and for more complex ends. Sir Arthur learned and practiced and learned from his few mistakes, for make no mistake, little Sir Arthur was not just small, he was smart. When the war came, Sir Arthur was a very important man in the purchase and routing of necessary equipment and armament. He built on what he had learned as a child—as a little child. The big ears of the little child became the spy networks of the military man. Officers and the wives of officers learned fear, and Sir Arthur learned power. The small man gained in wealth and importance. A small man still, and a small man always in his soul, but a man of great stature in his consequence and his growing wealth.

Even then, he still could not buy back his own land from the rotten colonials who had stolen his birthright on the hill. He could not find the hook for the fish. He could not learn enough!

So he bribed the staff—but only when he did not have the right information to blackmail them. Arthur was frugal in his dealings with the servants. Formerly, rightfully, they were his parents' servants. They should be his servants now. A man of his father's stature and class was expected to gamble on cards, on horses. He was expected to own horses and run them and bet on them. He was not expected to lose, continually to lose, terminally to lose. Until he lost his own home, his son's own home.

Sir Arthur had really been forced to marry this gawky carrot-topped nobody merely to get the land that was rightfully his. So he had every right to make her pay. It was only logical.

He still kept his staff of informants on the hill and in the town. However, they were small fry now compared to the system of informants now occupied all over Europe. These were the men he knew something about, the men he sold arms to, and all his useful friends all over Europe, and beyond—even further to the Middle

East. He caused to be made a rose garden on the sunny side of his new land by the road that led to High Place Old Lodge, all he could salvage of his birthright, and he set his lovely auburn-haired wife in the center of it so all his informants and all his struggling caught fish both could see her as they were driven up to High Place Old Lodge. Always the title in full. High Place Old Lodge. Preferably in caps.

Lady Riddecoombe made a lovely picture seen from the high windows of the library in the tastefully remodeled old home, really a mansion in itself. She impressed the self-made men who had married too soon in their upward movement or who had not yet acquired a younger, more attractive, wife as befit his new standing in this postwar world where the money flowed in slightly different more shadowed channels than before. They never brought their own wives to visit, of course. Wives weren't interested in business, were they? Envious men could see Sir Arthur's lovely wife out those spacious windows, in that spacious rose garden, and they could hate him.

It was fortunate for all concerned that neither party could hear the other. The small gatherings with their intense negotiations would have been aghast, in a gentlemanly way, as if the delicate Reynolds in its gilded frame on the wall over the fireplace had begun to curse them like a Hogarth's fishwife for what they were.

"Damn, and damn, and hellfire, and damnation." Lady Riddecoombe spoke her heartfelt words very quietly, as was so very necessary even in the quiet of the rose garden on the hill in the sun. Quiet they were, but there was no doubt that they came from the heart.

Lady Riddecoombe was still very busy with her correspondence, her pale blue gray stationery. She was not writing now, however. She was quietly and with great precision tearing up the delicate sheets and their delicate envelopes. They were good for writing congratulations to ladies she didn't know or condolences to ladies she didn't like, but not for writing as writing should be, full of images and ideas and fire and color and power. Full of life and laughter and freedom.

Up the hill came Braithwaite, the butler. He was of an age and heft that the trudge up the hill was not as quiet as he would have liked. He had perfected his butlerian sneak along spacious corridors—or not so spacious, if they were in the servants' quarters—but above all, along level corridors. Lady Riddecoombe, seeing his efforts with a certain unladylike glee, paused in her occupation and smiled at him. The aging butler had been brought to High Place Old Lodge by Sir Arthur when the old man had been dismissed by those at the top of the hill. Braithwaite, in his new position, was a reliable source of information to Sir Arthur. Being a source of information, possibly damaging information, was not a physically demanding position for a man of his years—except when it involved the climb to the rose garden on the hill.

"More letters, Braithwaite?"

"Yes, madam, always some little note, it seems."

Lady Riddecoombe rose. "I'll just take these to the conservatory then, since the sun seems to be deserting us once more."

Braithwaite bent slowly to the delicate little shreds of paper.

"Don't bother, Braithwaite. I'll have Brown help you clear all this away."

"Thank you, madam," he replied, gasping only slightly, and daringly seated himself on the same knobs and crockets upon which Lady Anne had so recently gracefully balanced herself. Damn. The breeze that had begun blowing with the changing of the light had blown all the little shreds of blue gray notepaper, catching them against the thorns of the rose bushes. Now he couldn't see what damaging evidence he might find valuable if brought to the right places. Those fragile little shreds, however, were innocent of any ink whatsoever. How was the butler to know that what Lady Riddecoombe had been destroying was the embossed name at the top of each page, Lady Anne Riddecoombe?

Chapter 4

A Change In The Weather

Anne spent many sunny days, and not a few cloudy days, in the rose garden. It was so very different from anything on the farm back in the States. She missed the zinnias and the cosmos and the mums in the fall—common flowers. She even missed the line of pumpkins that followed the flowers along the edge of the vegetable garden after the first light frosts. She was thinking, remembering all the details of those flowers so she could write about them later in her own room. She was remembering other details as well, details not related to flowers and pumpkins. It was impossible to tell that the lady was doing far more than merely posing to be seen through the tall windows of Sir Arthur's impressive library. She had a way of cocking her head slightly to one side as if she were listening to something no one else could hear. Arthur had been forced to speak to her about it several times. He should have paid more attention. That slight little movement meant that she was thinking about something. Not speaking. No. Arthur had been forced to speak to her many times about that as well until she became becomingly silent, with just the faintest of smiles like the portraits of the lovely ladies—ancestors, purchased recently by Sir Arthur, but painted long ago by famous artists, ladies who smiled just faintly because their teeth were so bad from all the dainty bonbons. Few artists dared to paint an open smile like Lady Riddecoombe's, like Ann's, open smile, when she could smile all alone in her pink and cream boudoir. No, she just sat and thought and made up stories about what she was seeing, looking down from the rose garden on the hill. She could see the lane as it curved up to the front of the lodge. She could also see all the cars that came and went to the impressive portico. Most of them were closed cars, so it was difficult to see within. The men who went from car to lodge and from lodge back to car again were puzzling to her ladyship, difficult to interpret in those too-brief moments. How can a man slink from a car door held open by a chauffeur to a lodge door held open by a large butler? Yet slink they did, or droop or drop resignedly into the plush upholstery. Why? The Ann who still lived within her ladyship had not yet realized that all that difficulty was intentional and full of purpose both for those who slunk and for Sir Arthur.

That secrecy was one of the things Anne thought about. Secrecy. Why such secrecy?

She knew that her husband, the thought was like a garter snake down her spine—and she knew exactly what that felt like from personal experience—her husband was a man dealing in high finance, international in scope. She knew that many of these men were men he had become acquainted with in the higher ranks of the military. The war was over, was it not? Surely the time for secrecy was over? No? If not, why not? She tried to recognize any of these strangely secret men. She even began to look at the newspapers to see if any of them were pictured there. No. Never. Even the men in Near Eastern garb, men whose appearance in this country would have made news, she thought. News, possibly, but never pictures. Never something that a person in the man's native country would recognize in a picture, even if he didn't know the words. So she began to ponder reasons. Why should they be so secret? She never, ever asked. Then she wondered why she didn't. It did not take long to realize that Arthur's business was his alone.

Very occasionally, she overheard conversations. From time to time, Sir Arthur would talk with one of the local men. Very occasionally there were women too, one especially, who would come. Lady Riddecoombe never saw them enter or leave the house. Of course they would use the servants' entrance on the far side of the house near the service areas of the lodge. Sometimes Arthur would raise his voice and sound very, very angry. The speaking would stop altogether then, and that voice would not be heard again for a long, long time—if ever. Where had the voice gone? Had the voice a family? A position? A position no longer? Arthur was not as careful to keep his voice down when talking to these local people. Country folk. He should have been more careful.

As Ann began to wonder who these people were, she began to wonder who she was.

Now there was a question! Who was she? Who had she become and why?

She knew, or thought she knew, that she was Lady Anne Riddecoombe, wife of Sir Arthur Riddecoombe. That seemed to be enough for Arthur. That in itself was strange. Why was it enough for her? Was it enough? Her own thought, 'absolutely not,' sounded so loudly in her ears that it made her jump. Cautiously, her ladyship glanced around her like a guilty child fearing—fearing what? She felt like a child hearing a terrifying children's fairy tale. That fairy tale, terrifying as it was, was her life!

The more she thought, the less she knew. What was she for? Was she accomplishing anything? No, absolutely not. Surely she had recovered from the losses and the grief of war. It was not the deaths of her parents. Yet it felt like grief. Why? If she were still in the States, what would she be doing? What would she be accomplishing? Would she have married one of her foster brothers? Lord, no! What a thought! Then what? Unconsciously, her head started to tilt as it had before, in school on an essay exam. Topic: What was her purpose? What was her future?

Memories flooded back, memories bright with color and movement! Yellow writing pads. She wouldn't just be thinking. She would be writing! She should have understood when she was tearing up that forsaken stationery! She needed paper she could put thoughts on! What sort of fog had she been in these almost three years now! Years in amber. She would use the questions she had asked herself about the men who had come and gone, write the questions and then write out all the possibilities. She would watch them with a purpose now! She felt shame. Jane Austen had written wonderfully about the kind of life she was leading, hadn't she? Jane Austen hadn't been married to Arthur. Lucky Jane. That was no excuse! What would Jane Austen have made of the life of Lady Anne Riddecoombe? Now there was a topic!

Could she write living where she was now? The question was not could she write. She knew she could. At least she had known. The more disturbing question had to be, was it safe to write where she was now? Could she write about where she was now, still living where she was now? What would Arthur say? Because he would find out. That was not even a question. He would find out. Arthur would not like her writing about his friends, his business acquaintances, rather. Again, that was not even a question. How much would he not like it? Quite a lot? Dangerously so? Why did she think of danger? She hadn't really been in danger her whole life, had she? Not real danger. That was why her parents had sent her to the States during the war wasn't it, to keep her out of danger? Why was she frightened now? Because she was frightened. Again, that was not a question. There was grief, yes, she had been right about that. Much more important was the thing she had missed seeing—the fear. Fear in herself and fear in the men she watched. No, she could not write here.

Chapter 5

Storm Front

As she began to look at Arthur more closely, she could see that the games he played with his "friends," with his business acquaintances, closely resembled the ones he so enjoyed playing with her. He studied his play prey closely, seeming always to be so interested in their ideas, their views. There was Sir Arthur, listening so attentively, always homing in on the little lacunae of character, tweaking the vulnerable spots. Learning what hurt and what was ignored. He was best at it playing with people who were bullies, but he had a curious sideline in hurting those who wanted most to please him. The vulnerabilities were so obvious! Whatever they invested themselves in most, were most anxious to please him with, those things he rejected most strongly, with most contempt. It was an easy game. Kid stuff. Literally stuff he had learned as a kid. It was the way he controlled his small circle of admirers, the ones who were bullied by the bigger, meaner, and often most self-enamored and pompous ones. The ones whose circle of vision included only themselves. The empty ones. Those were the big game. The ones who bullied and then bragged, not even seeing the ones who were watching them and remembering them and what they had said. It had always come as such a delicious thrill to watch them as they realized they had been seen and heard. They had been seen saying and doing just those things that their own aristocratic families rejected most in others. That *their* Archibald or Terrance or Clyde or even Alicia would do such a thing—and be seen by witnesses, or more specifically by a witness, by this witness who wrote such a polite, condescending little note explaining just what he could explain to the headmaster or the games mistress at that other school if he were of a mind. And he would be of such a mind, unless—well. He was sure they understood, didn't they? They understood.

That was the big game. The lesser game were the ones who gathered around Arthur, as they thought, for protection. The confiding ones. The weak ones. The gains in material value might not be as high as the, well, not really blackmail, but say, information passed to those who could pay well to keep it from seeing the light of day. More specifically, the light on the headmaster's desk. No, the smaller prey were just the little games played for the fun of the pain and terror they caused. Really just games rather than the business, but never blackmail—no, never call it blackmail!—played for higher stakes with players of higher standing and bigger pockets. Take the housemaids he had started his training with or the butlers he knew could be brought to a fine sweat just by letting them know that what they knew, he knew too. Letting a butler who had been watering the wine rather too heavily know that he knew too, and if they chose to pay him not to pass along the surely understandable but possibly misunderstood slip to his master, he was more than willing to come to an agreement. That did not, never did mean, that he would forget entirely. Surely that was impossible.

No, he was playing for very high international stakes now. With ambassadors. With clerks of embassies, with playboy sons of those with interests in the business of steel and commodities as well as diamonds and, especially, armaments.

The little ones became boring after a while. The bigger ones had lasting interest.

Arthur smiled at that. "Lasting interest." Words were funny things, weren't they?

They could mean so many different things. So many *interesting* things.

Still, since he was back, close to if not on his own home ground, he must ask—no, he must tell Miss Tilly to take tea with Mrs. Dray more often. It would be fun to renew old ties. To establish new controls. Petty, perhaps, but just something to relieve the boredom.

Chapter 6

Disappointing Conditions

Speaking of boredom, there was his wife. His very obedient wife, so eager to please. So crushed by failure. Not knowing that it was exactly by this failure that he was best pleased. The delightful slouch! The lovely clothes stretched and pulled at the seams by that slouch. Trying so hard to get *down to his level*. Oh, the delight of it! Each migraine was a little triumph. Just look at this pathetic attempt to show an interest in the local school, established in honor of his grandfather and funded by himself! How touching. What a vulnerable spot. Was she really helping the little brats, or was she merely raising false hopes in their forever-to-be-little minds? The doubts he could insert into those little lacunae of vulnerability. Doubts and fears he could tend and watch grow! Still, there was a certain monotony creeping in after three years. A migraine was, after all, just a migraine, and certainly not an heir. Perhaps the tender concern for her health might be ratcheted up a bit. The loving suggestion that a vacation at one of the more highly recommended exclusive sanatoria could be inserted into the conversation and into the vulnerable soft spot of her soul. Her soul? Was that her weakness? Did she, in fact, have a soul? Or think she had? Was she burdened with a conscience? How dull. Was she really beginning to bore him so much that a question like that would enter his mind? He wondered.

While Arthur wondered, Anne developed her interest in the local school further and further. She had begun the project with one goal in her mind. She needed lined paper—reams of lined paper. Ann began by being the donor of writing materials to the local Riddecoombe School and keeping some of it for herself—something not too unlike the techniques her husband had used in the military supplies departments he oversaw. However, for the sake of her conscience, she paid for what she took. She suggested topics for the writing classes. Topics such as what did they want their futures to be? Not "What do I want to be when I grow up?" The answers to which would predictably be "I want to be a farmer like my dad," or "a maid at the big house up on the hill," or just possibly "I want to be a teacher like Miss Appleby." Being a teacher like Mary Appleby or a nurse like her sister, Nurse Martha Appleby, would make good role models for these girls, girls who so seldom had any other role in their heads than that of wife and mother. Wife and mother were good roles, useful roles, but by choice, not by default. She asked herself the questions she was asking the children. "How can I make myself useful to the world?" Even "What would I change?" And then "How would I go about it?"

Miss Appleby had to be brought into the project early on and eased into it slowly and with great patience. Well, Anne had the greatest of patience. Fair was fair; she was asking herself the same questions. Sometimes the answers seemed incredible to the children and to herself. "How could I get there from here?"

Anne's headaches became less and less, and yet she spent more and more time in her room with them. This gave Arthur and his staff the impression that they were, in fact, becoming worse and worse. Which was just what she wanted them to think.

Still, she couldn't get past that most important question: "Can I get there from here?"

She knew where *there* was. *There* was "out." It was "away from here!" Away from Arthur, away from High Place Old Lodge. She was developing the real migraines again. She loved the West Country. She was coming to love the old Riddecoombe School and its children, but she had to have freedom. As much freedom as she could have and still support herself until she could find a way to write full-time. The more she saw of the faces coming and going to and from High Place Old Lodge, the more she heard the sudden silences, the more she knew she had to be away from this place before her face looked like those seen briefly in and out of the cars that came and went, constantly came and went.

She looked in her mirror, her gold and white full length rococo mirror and was stunned. She already had the face of those nonpeople! What more could she fear? That was when she heard the muffled rumors and the stifled gossip beyond her door, beyond the green baize door. Suicide. One of those nonpeople had killed himself!

No. Definitely not! It was all a misunderstanding. An error in reporting. A man too long away from his homeland. Personal problems. He had been having severe headaches.

Terrible headaches.

Migraines.

I am getting out.

Chapter 7

Sudden Squalls

Ann was furious! Absolutely furious! Her face flamed so that it glowed in sympathy with her rich auburn hair. He hadn't cared! Arthur had not cared twopence! All her rehearsals! All her lists of possible demands, requests, pleadings!

"Of course, my dear. I've often thought of it myself. You made too large a change too quickly, didn't you? I had wondered, you know. You couldn't handle all the new responsibilities, could you? Perfectly understandable. A separation would calm your nerves, wouldn't it? Your very fragile nerves! Finances will be no problem, no problem at all! Of course, with the style of life you are accustomed to, there will be no question of a major imposition on the estate!

"Would you like to take Marie with you? No? Ah, the French language has always confused you, hasn't it! So accustomed to the American slang. I'll have the estate lawyers start working on it immediately! Why not get a breath of fresh air in the garden now? I do have visitors expected any minute, and yes, for dinner, but they will understand your absence, of course.

"Here, just before you go, let me see your list of suggestions. Ah, yes, I see no problems, or very few, at least. The wording is a little childish, of course, but the meaning is clear enough. Now, if you will excuse me? Some time in the garden perhaps. The fresh air should help bring those roses back, don't you think?"

It was like missing a step in the dark! All the effort! All the fear and trembling!

Damn him! Damn him! Damn him!

And yet for what? For giving her what she wanted? Just like that? What was the thing she'd missed? There had to have been something she'd missed. Missing it could be dangerous. She couldn't think. What? What? What?

What she didn't know was that she had made him furious!

Yes, he had gotten just what he wanted! Of course he had. He always did.

The insult was that *she* had asked him!

He hadn't told her!

Damn her! Damn her! Damn her!

Through the tall windows in his library, he could see his wife storming up the hill to the rose garden. Oh, that unfortunate country wife stride! Oh well. At least he was the one who owned her country now. Let her go.

Time enough to call his own back to him—his little piggy bank out there in the wide world of temptation. She would probably buy a nice flat in London where his agents could keep a watch as she yielded—the pun amused him—interest. Then when his little piggy bank was caught by incriminating evidence of adultery, she could be brought back to him and broken open, as all piggy banks were in the end. That was what they were for after all, wasn't it?

That the evidence would come, he had no doubt. She was young. He had trained her to be dependent. Of course she would not be able to support herself. Had he not trained her to need the lovely gowns even as he had trained her to stand and walk so they looked like nothing on earth? Had he not trained her to think that it had all been her fault, this gaucherie? He had given her enough and yet not enough. Surely it was only a matter of time until—how did they say it now? Yes, she would become needy. Just as surely that meant, in Arthur's mind, that she would need a man. Oh yes, his little piggy bank would fill with evidence for a lovely scandalous divorce case, real or potential, he didn't really care which. The joy was that *she* would care! Oh yes, she would. This, however, was another of the little games. It could wait. Meanwhile, another dark car with dark windows had stopped at the door of High Place Old Lodge.

Chapter 8

Too Much Sun

There is a thing called eustress. It means literally an overload of glorious stress. It can disorient the human mind as much as stress over a disaster. More, it can divide the mind's responses against itself. Is it happy? Then why the stress? Is it sad? Then why this overwhelming sense of freedom? Is it really freedom? Or will there be another stone after you've worn away the stone you can see in the prison wall after you laboriously scraped away the first one with your laboriously sharpened spoon? Possibly a little note, perhaps from a cadre of estate lawyers mentioning this or that little, very little, change in the wording of this or that, which could mean all the difference between the freedom she had anticipated and a return to the captivity she dreaded.

Ann was mired ankle-deep in eustress. If she pulled one foot out of its boot, where would she put that foot while she pulled the other foot to freedom? It felt very much like mucking out the pig styes back home. Was that where she was going? No! She had been over this already, remember?

Home was the West Country, but the West Country of England. Here was home. She knew the ways of it, the bird songs of it, the seasons. Further, she wanted to be close to the Riddecoombe School, close enough to visit and to watch the children she had come to know so well find their way to their own futures. Most of all, it was the land. The feel of it under her feet. The chalk from under the sea. Soft chalk, yes, but with hidden flint, hard, sharp, and enduring flint. The downs swelling like great green waves under a huge and endless sky. This was freedom, this was life, this was home.

In this, at the very least, the very least, Arthur had been very wrong about his lady.

London, with its blackened hole in the ground, had been home once. No more.

So she turned to the ads in the newspapers. She walked and walked and took this bus and that bus. Her family had always done whatever was in front of them by themselves for themselves, and that was the only plan she had. She had been brought up to buy only what she could afford to pay at that immediate time. Hiring an agent would have been anathema to her parents. One did not pay for what one could do for oneself. So she studied maps and read advertisements and walked and rode busses until she was exhausted. Finally she noticed that the signs in front of the houses that she liked all had the same logo on them along with a phone number. Here were professional people who did what she was trying to do every day, who made their living at—what did they call it? Selling houses at any rate.

After a few weeks of walking and staring through bus windows, she received a letter from the estate lawyers confirming the finality of all those papers she had signed and if she would only please come in, at her convenience, of course, and sign the final papers, her account would be set up at the bank she had chosen, and she would be able to draw on the account.

So at her own convenience, of course, she signed all the papers set before her and went with one of the lawyers to the bank of her choice, and lo and behold, she was a woman she could call well-off. Well-off and free! So long as she still called herself Lady Anne Riddecoombe.

Chapter 9

Some Sun At Midday

Separation meant living apart. In 1952 England, it did not mean divorce.

She shuddered to think—had shuddered at the thought of what trying to get a divorce from Arthur would have meant. Nevertheless, *Ann* sounded enough like *Anne* to make the difference slight enough, and *Lady* gave no indication of marital status.

Ann, as she at long last thought of herself, remembered the phone number on the placards in front of the homes she had liked the best. She called Herrick, Makepeace, and Herrick and, after fumbling with a very new vocabulary with the aid of a very patient receptionist, arranged to meet with the "younger Mr. Herrick" the next afternoon. So she was being given a Mr. Herrick, was she? Ann imagined it had been the *Lady* that had been particularly persuasive in giving her one of the owners to introduce her to the world of buying houses. This was going to be a bit tricky, thought plain Ann as she walked into the pleasant room reserved for important prospects. The receptionist introduced herself as Barbara. Settling Ann in a comfortable chair, she gave Lady Riddecoombe a brochure of all the listings a lady might be interested in. Young Mr. Herrick, it seemed, was temporarily held up with other clients.

Ann had been right. These were homes far beyond her needs or her wishes. Barbara abandoned her typing and began a pleasant conversation. Ann suspected that for Barbara, *refined* was a verb. Barbara had refined herself into a model receptionist for a well-respected firm. Barbara, as she had begun, probably would have had a much closer resemblance to the barmaid who had served the Laughing Cavalier. She had not left herself to herself and, Ann had to admit, had done a very passable job of refining herself into upward mobility. She was a natural blonde and had left it at that. No streaking or expensive do. Wise woman. Arthur had found it inexplicable that Ann had not maintained her glossy auburn do.

Ann learned a good deal from Barbara about the arcane vocabulary of the selling or renting—this said on a slightly lower tone of voice—of homes, not houses, not on the other hand "places of abode." By the time young Mr. Herrick finally said good-bye to the large family he had been so patient with, Ann felt much more at ease and could look forward to the encounter before her.

Young Mr. Herrick, therefore, came as a surprise. He looked both younger and older than she had expected. He was certainly older than she, but not by as much as she had thought at first glance. Very well dressed, but quietly so. Tall. Straight, but straight, it seemed, with an effort. His hair was the blond of beech tree leaves in winter, yet it was not gray. He himself seemed gray. He limped a little, something Ann put down to the war years without quite knowing why. Something about the way he held himself. His eyes were a darker gray in a face thinner than it should have been. He was tall. Taller than Ann. A man she could look up to. She had to look up to him, and that made her smile. That took him back a little. Was he not used to being smiled at? He seemed to be missing something, to have lost something. It came almost as a blow to Ann. It was not something he had lost, though there was that too. He *was* lost—lost and adrift and cold and exhausted.

Ann's sympathy seemed to come to him from across the room. He stumbled a bit as he came toward them, but his self-control returned instantly as Barbara made the introductions. Lady Riddecoombe, of course. The three of them went over the brochure Barbara had given Lady Riddecoombe, and they talked about the properties she might want to view. Also, very discreetly of course, what she might want to pay. Barbara's contributions were light, cheerful, and perceptive. Mr. Herrick's were calm, courteous, and even more perceptive.

As they talked, he made notes in his portfolio, frowning a little as he did so. "I really don't expect a soul-to-soul matching, at least not quickly, but I'm sure we'll find something that will suit you very well. Would you be willing to love a less finished home that would cost less but be sound and respond well to your own personal renovations? Something that would eventually suit you perfectly?"

Oh, he knew his field, did Mr. Herrick. Further, and very unsettling, he also seemed to know Ann surprisingly well. Not Lady Riddecoombe, but Ann. This she was definitely not expecting. She was surprised that being known this well in this short and painless period had been not at all threatening but really rather pleasant. She was further surprised when he rose and asked, "May I suggest that we discuss the possibilities further over a not-so-early lunch at the Green Goose? At least partly as an apology for my tardiness to our appointment?" Taking a speechless Ann by the elbow, Mr. Herrick graciously led her out the door and into the sunshine.

The Green Goose was very comfortable with itself, and it was impossible for Ann not to be comfortable in its cheerful atmosphere. It had been there for many years and saw no reason not to think of itself as continuing on for many more, with crisp red curtains at its bottle-glass windows and its bright red geraniums in plain pots at the open door. The smells of home-brewed beer and fresh-baked bread, so much alike, blended to make an aroma that made any newcomers realize how hungry and/or thirsty they were. It was stimulating and relaxing at the same time.

The innkeeper of the Green Goose was Mr. Green. This was a bit of local humor enjoyed by his many customers. He seemed pleased to see the two of them. Ann was not to know that a good part of his pleasure came from seeing Mr. Herrick at the Green Goose with a charming young woman. They "went well" together, he told his wife later. As he watched them come down the cobbled road, the innkeeper had noticed the lack of the limp that had plagued young Mr. Herrick for so long. This pleased Mr. Green as well, and the man, more perceptive than the expected jovial innkeeper, was not slow to make the connection.

During the easy stroll down the street to the Green Goose, Ann had also been aware that Mr. Herrick's leg seemed to have stopped bothering him. Ann thought it would be interesting to notice when it became troublesome. He had certainly stumbled when he first saw her at the office. She also wondered what would sooth his pain. Stop it! Mr. Herrick was helping her find a home where she could enjoy being alone and independent. It was his job to help people buy and sell homes. What could be more natural?

What was she thinking? She took herself in hand to restore her own balance. Mr. Herrick seemed content with the natural quiet leisure as they strolled down the cobbled street, and Ann was well back in control by the time they were comfortably seated in the cool dimly lit old inn.

Mr. Herrick was a gracious host and a subtle interrogator. Ann gradually became convinced that this Mr. Herrick knew much more about her than Sir Arthur ever had. Oddly, she still was not threatened by this, even though she had only been alone with one man for three years. Three years! Three years best forgotten.

Whatever he found out about Ann, he accepted. What he was finding out about Sir Arthur, though she mentioned him only briefly, added to Mr. Herrick's already growing disgust of the man. He had met the type before all too often. However, he concealed his emotional reaction well—for the most part.

Certainly his approval for Ann herself and for her search for a new home and a new life to live in it came through well enough. Ann was able to relax even more. *Heavens,* she thought, *I must have a long way to go towards a really comfortable kind of relaxation if this is what it takes to relax the muscles of the shoulders and make a smile really natural.*

She waited for an easy opening in the conversation and then said, "Please, could we make it just plain Ann?"

He couldn't hear that the *e* had dropped as well.

"As you know by now, my former life was—well, the whole point of the new house is a new life, and I intend to be Lady Riddecoombe only in formal situations and on paper."

Mr. Herrick nodded. "Ann it is then." And he hesitated as he was going to add the now forbidden "my lady." He smiled as they both realized the reason for the hesitation.

He's coming along nicely, she thought, *not really considering where he might be headed in his coming along.* She was coming along as well. When she had her freedom, might she consider their courses further? Too soon, much too soon.

She realized how little she knew about him. He was her agent, charged with locating this new home, but not really a guest in that home yet. Perhaps a friendship would grow, perhaps not. Something Barbara had mentioned, just casually in passing, had given Ann the impression that the young Mr. Herrick was a bachelor. His private life, she almost thought of it as his former life, was as far away from her as her own former life was. All she could tell now was that he had the potential to be a very vital young man behind that very stony gray control. Firm, strong, but not in any way harsh. Ann thought he would make a convincing hero in one of her books. Ann knew firsthand the energy it took to maintain that kind of control. She recognized it as control, not ease, although he was very good at the deception. Was that deception intentional? Was it a part of his professional image? She would watch this enigmatic man. She felt they had much in common.

Ann could remember vividly the strength she had needed to confront Sir Arthur and the long years—only three?—of combined fear and boredom that had been her life with him. She had heard soldiers talking about the combination of fear and boredom repeated again and again, fear and then boredom, fear and then boredom, that had been so much a part of the lives of the soldiers at the front. Add anger and frustration, and one had a kind of Four Horsemen. *What were his Four Horsemen?* she wondered. She hoped they were in the past, to be slowly and steadily forgotten, and not still present behind the very control that marked their existence.

"Ann. Come back. There are better places to dwell."

Abruptly, Ann returned to find herself seated in the comfortable old inn with Mr. Herrick looking at her with a deep and gentle concern that took her breath away. She refused to give the usual bromides for absentmindedness, but she could drink the cold well water slowly and breathe slowly and focus on something safe. She found herself focusing on Mr. Herrick's hand, long-fingered and smoothly muscled, resting on the table next to her own.

It was a smiling Ann who thanked Mr. Herrick for their pleasant lunch as they walked back to the office. She was comfortable being a lady, if not a Lady, and knew she would not return to the days when she could be a tomboy out in the fields and in the orchard. Still, an orchard, just a small one, might be pleasant by this new home. She would be patient and see what was offered.

After picking up his portfolio and some house keys, Mr. Herrick handed her into the front seat of the large new car that was part of the tools of his trade. The backseat was still a little sticky from the happy family who had been his previous clients.

Chapter 10

Possibly Pleasant Weather Following

"A few are a little bit farther out, but there are one or two that might be promising."

Ann sat quietly watching this land that she realized she had come to love so much. She felt she was sharing in its springtime, its renewal. She wondered if any of these "promising" new homes had gardens. Not that she needed a ready-made garden, she realized. It would be her home, and she could create her own garden! It would not be a rose garden. Her—*her*—new garden would have flowers that could take care of themselves. Her long-ago home in London had not really had a garden. She found that she liked the idea of having a garden of her own, with plants that grew on sturdy stems and that didn't need sprays or fertilizers that came in colorful plastic bags from a floral shop.

"You will note, I hope," said Mr. Herrick, breaking into her visions, "I am not showing you a series of hopeless ruins first so that you will appreciate the charms of the ultimate property. I like this first one. Of course, we could visit the ruins later, if you like." He smiled briefly. "This one has been vacant since the end of the war—a dispute between the heirs over the will—but the property is free and clear now and has been kept up by our company, so it is still sound, if not paint perfect. Most of it is hidden under considerable dust, however. The woman we have in charge of the place is not a good housekeeper. It would help the company enormously if you would take her off our hands. Not, really not, by hiring her! Lord, what a thought. You are not allergic to dust, are you? I mean, really allergic?"

Ann shook her head. She was listening now, intently. If this was the house he liked, what would he say about the others?

"All dry rot has been repaired, of course, and things replaced that were obviously missing. You'll notice where the woodwork and plaster have been repaired and replaced. They did a good job that way, but it has been left unpainted, "awaiting the wishes of the new owner.""

Ann was becoming accustomed to his unspoken quotation marks and enjoyed sharing the humor behind them.

"At one time the family of old man Thatcher, the man who had lived here for some time, employed a 'maid of all work,' read drudge who avoided all work, who had lived out, and a very good groundskeeper who lived in, if you call living over the stables in. The man was good with his hands and had made himself a very comfortable living quarters there. He left to enlist shortly before the war and hasn't been seen since. All we know is that he received an honorable discharge. We could try to find him for you, if you like."

Ann noticed the assumption, if he did not. This was not a property she could handle by herself.

"The drudge married her man just as he was called up. The house will need a significant amount of drudgery to get it to where you want it, but it will get there. That is, if you take to it at all."

Mr. Herrick truly sounded shy. He had suddenly come to the realization that he had been seeing her in this house of his. All his planning and preparation might not be enough to convince her that she belonged there. Who was he to say with such certainty that she would?

Then she saw it.

Ann sat forward, looking intently at a house just under the brow of a hill. Tidy rather than graceful in its lines, of a pleasing rose brick with what could be white trim, or would cream be better with the rose of the brick? Two large bay windows, possibly an afterthought, had been let into the facade on each side of the front door. The wide curving front steps completed the effect of a smiling face with powerful glasses. The windows behind them were blinded. The blinds could be removed. She could—oh, the possibilities!

Ann looked at Mr. Herrick. She had been unaware that he had pulled over onto the verge and was looking at her. "Yes?" Her voice was hopeful, almost to the point of pleading.

"Yes," he answered. "Would you like to see inside? I've brought the keys." He sounded hopeful as well, as if suddenly he had realized that this might not have happened even though he had seen it in his mind's eye so very clearly.

"Oh please!" Ann had an inborn native habit of openness, of optimism. Comparing the joy in her voice now to the subdued voice of the shy young woman he had met in the office of Herrick, Makepeace, and Herrick told him just how nearly Sir Arthur had killed that joy. Perhaps working on this house might even work to restore Ann at the same time. Mr. Herrick also could hope.

"Could we go in through the garden?"

Garden? There was space for a garden—for a flower garden. The larger space, presumably for vegetables, was to the side of the house. Yet Ann had seen a garden here. The legal wrangling over the separation had continued well into summer, and the "garden" they were standing in now was in full bloom, such as there was of it. It was a tangle of untended greens with a few flowers: blues, reds, and some faded whites hanging on stems that clung or drooped. Most of the flowers had faded already. It did not impress Mr. Herrick, but Ann seemed enthralled.

"Oh, look! Love-in-a-mist!"

Mr. Herrick looked at the untamed tangle around him. Then he looked at Ann.

"The little light blue flower with leaves like dill. You do know dill?"

Mr. Herrick did know dill.

"Well, when the flowers are blooming in the midst of the mist—those slender light green leaves—people call it love-in-a-mist. Later, like now, when the seed pod expands like a little balloon and grows horns at the top, people call it devil-in-a-bush."

Chapter 11

Cold Front

This was possibly the wrong time to notice Mrs. Dray.

Mrs. Dray was employed, and shortly to be terminated in that employment, both by the heirs and by Mr. Herrick's agency, neither of whom knew the other was paying her a salary. The heirs couldn't have cared less. You could call her the caretaker of the property, if the results of any care were there to be seen. As it was, she was simply there.

She stood in the open door of the little house, like an evil icon of the neglect the house had suffered. She was short and, well, fat. Not to beat around the bush; it didn't take much imagination to see her as the devil in that bush. Her round head was far too small for her much larger but still round body. Her hair was relentlessly dragged back to a small round bun at the back of the small round head. Her eyes were small and black. If the eyes were the windows of the soul, as the Victorian writers would have it, that soul was dark as a cavern. Her mouth was small and pursed and looked greedy, as if she were trying to suck the world into that black cavern and never to let anything out. Not even a moth.

Mrs. Dray had not heard the car come up the sparsely graveled drive since the two had walked up on the grass, and she considered herself snuck up upon. She made no attempt to disguise her disapproval.

Mr. Herrick accepted her disapproving silence and politely returned it to the woman.

Ann smiled, making an enemy for life.

"I assume you did not receive my message." Mr. Herrick was not really asking a question.

"Well, the phone bill wasn't paid, was it?"

I'm sure if you looked closely at your contract, you would notice that the bill was to have been covered by your remuneration. The responsibility was yours." Mr. Herrick turned apologetically to Ann. "Lady Riddecoombe, my sincere apologies. Would you still like to view the premises?"

The "Lady Riddecoombe" should have sounded a bell of some kind with Mrs. Dray. A bell did sound. It told Mrs. Dray that here was a possible source of information useful to her former employer. Mrs. Dray was a gossip. She was a professional only in that she expected to be paid.

Her ladyship smiled warmly at Mr. Herrick. "Thank you. I would like that very much." Ann walked graciously past Mrs. Dray and into the dimly lit house.

"And the electricity bill, Mrs. Dray?"

Wordlessly, Mrs. Dray turned on what lights still had bulbs in them, making the rooms slightly less dismal. She sniffed disapprovingly. It was a mistake. The dust had been roused to nose level by this time, and she had no possible way to avoid sneezing.

Ann walked quickly and, for her, noisily into the large kitchen, hoping to cover not Mrs. Dray's sneeze but Lady Riddecoombe's snort of laughter.

She stopped as she got her first glimpse of the large, dismal, gray, and completely dust covered room. With the eye of the true writer, she could see, not the room in front of her, but the room as it could be. The room as it would be if she had anything to do with its future. This room in her mind's eye was lovely. The musty blinds were gone. Sunshine, or at least fresh air, flowed through open windows and lit the creams and roses and light sky blues of the slipcovers on comfortable chairs, the gently blowing curtains, the braided rug on the polished floor, and the polish on the gleaming pans hanging, ready to be used over the fire on the hearth. Blue stoneware and cream crockery were neatly placed on the polished counters, and the huge old oak table was ready for her to bake and . . . and . . . and do whatever she wanted to do in her kitchen. There was even a cat by the hearth. Ann wondered briefly if Mr. Herrick was allergic to cats.

"The other room, the one across the hall, I imagine, was used as a parlor of sorts?" Ann crossed the broad dim hall that divided the main floor in half and ended in a door at the back of the house. Yes, it had been the parlor, when it had been used at all. Christenings, weddings, and funerals alone had filled this room with guests, the funerals being the aura that lingered longest. No, it was probably its use as a sick room for the long dreary time before the old man's final passing had doomed this room to eternal gloom. Even Ann's eye had trouble with this room—until her mind's eye saw the large table, not as large as the kitchen's, but still generous with the empty horizontal space so precious to a working writer. The typewriter was surrounded with reams of paper, and the pencils, scissors, erasers, and all the paraphernalia of writing were there. The chair, of course, was just the right height for her comfort at the typewriter. Now her eye was free to roam over the comfortable chairs, the sofa, the tables and—and the bookcases! Oh, the bookcases! All in her mind's eye, of course. All potential. All perfect.

Ann composed herself and turned to find Mr. Herrick smiling at her. She raised her chin and smiled right back, meaning it, and caught his startled hesitancy. It had not been a suggestive smile, just an accepting smile. Still, it seemed too much. Territory too new, too strange for him. Smiling a second longer to let him know she recognized his fear and was not made fearful herself by it, Ann walked out of the room and looked up the narrow stairs to the first floor. She knew she would buy the house. A first floor full of rattlesnakes would not have kept her from buying this house. Her curiosity was a very basic part of Ann, and she followed where it led. She also had to have Mr. Herrick—he had to have a first name, didn't he?—behind her for a minute. She had seen, in her writing inner sanctum, Mr. Herrick sitting comfortably at ease, reading in the soft glow of the lamp by the big chair across the room. Her room. For the second time that day, Ann had found her equilibrium upset by this quiet young man.

Chapter 12

Dust Storm

Carefully, Ann went up the dusty stairs to the first floor. As with the ground floor, the first floor had been conceived of as better only because bigger, merely a repetition of the ground floor. The two rooms above, as the two rooms below, each had a small fireplace, the ones in the upper rooms directly above the ones on the ground floor. All very sensible, all very to be expected. However, a curious slice had been cut out of the west room at a later time, walled off to create a bathroom of sorts. This had obviously been made without any of the integrity of style and workmanship that marked the rest of the house. Curiously, while the bathroom slice paralleled the side wall, it did not continue to the far wall, stopping a few feet short of it. Was it the work of builders not familiar with plumbing above the ground floor? Or with plumbing at all? Were the inept builders planning to put a closet there?

Ann was used to closets. Houses in the States, except for very old ones, had closet space. They had been a new invention, like interior staircases, that had marked a significant improvement from the eras of architecture that had gone before. Might this tiny unfinished square of rough lath and plaster be an incipient closet? It was dark and windowless and seemed to Ann destined only to be a small utterly inadequate closet. However, in the dim light, Ann could make out a kind of ladder on one side of the wall. It seemed to be made mostly of simple short rough pieces of lath nailed clumsily to the uprights. Not a closet then? Ann knew—she knew absolutely—that she should not try to climb this poor excuse for a ladder.

Mr. Herrick had stayed below briefly to read Mrs. Dray a short lecture on what had been expected of her, and why it was no longer being expected of her, and how soon she could leave.

Now Mr. Herrick followed Ann up into the dim dusty first floor.

Ann. Where was Ann? The rooms were simple squares with the exception of the strange growth that seemed to be a bathroom. That was soon explored and still revealed no Ann.

God! Where could she be? War images blurred his vision and his reason.

"Ann! Ann, where are you?"

Ann, now of course in the rough crawl space above, could hear him but could not understand the harshness of his voice. Was he angry? What had she done?

"Hello?"

Quickly, she stumbled to the hole in the floor and tried to hurry down the rough ladder, the stupidly rough ladder. Did they want people up there or not? Why put a ladder to nowhere? "Here I am!" Her hurry to reach Allen put more pressure on the unstable first rung than it could deal with, and Ann heard a mushy parting sound as the rung left the wall and crumbled onto the floor beneath.

Mr. Herrick had just reached the bottom of the treacherous ladder and was looking up in the dim light in hopes of catching sight of

Ann. Instead, he caught Ann, or tried to. She could not fall gracefully but fell catching her back along the rough bare lath and plaster of the wall in back of her and landing hard enough for him to break her fall, but not his own.

Rolling over out of the tightly enclosed space, he held her close as if she were a precious fragile piece of porcelain or a football to be defended against all comers. Ann, knowing herself to be something between the two, rolled off and sat up, coughing. Mr. Herrick rolled up on his elbows also coughing with the dust that choked him after Ann had knocked what good air he had had out of him with her fall.

The sight of agent and client gasping and laughing with dust swirling around them suggested many things to Mrs. Dray as she finally heaved herself up to the top of the stairs. She chose the one that shocked and delighted her most, of course. The one most useful to her. "Well, I never!" She stood on the step eye level with the floor on which all that ambiguous action had taken place. None of this was ambiguous to Mrs. Dray, however. "How you dared! And with me just exactly right beneath you the whole time!"

It eventually came to her that the two apparently consenting adults were clinging to each other more for support than from passion. They were gasping because they were laughing so hard. Mr. Herrick's eyes were glinting with mischief, not ardor. Mrs. Dray noticed too late that the mischief was rapidly turning into cold anger as he turned to look at her. Lady Riddecoombe's face was firmly pressed into Mr. Herrick's shoulder. Even Mrs. Dray could see that Lady Riddecoombe was shaking violently and was truly in need of this support. Her dress was badly torn, not by groping, passionate hands, but by cold rough lath and plaster. Her back was ripped and bloody.

Still a mystery here, Mrs. Dray thought hopefully. Surely this was something Sir Arthur would want to know about. Then Lady Riddecoombe raised her flushed, laughing face to his and coughed. "Oh my! What a dust up!" They collapsed against each other one more time, coughing, but laughing too, like children.

Mrs. Dray began the long slow descent to the floor below.

After the laughter slowed and stopped, Ann realized that her back was not as it should be. Numb at first, it began to sting rather than tingle. Then the tingle turned to serious pain and was growing more painful by the moment. Still supporting her, Mr. Herrick turned her slowly to survey the damage. The laughter drained from his face as he realized how bad it was. Ann tried to turn to see as well, but somehow that didn't work. She fainted.

"You need a thorough cleaning and about a hundred stitches." He tried to bring her around with his light tone. That didn't work either. He knew just how bad that pain would be when she regained consciousness and didn't try to bring her round any further. He winced and automatically blocked off memories as he had learned to do.

Then Ann stirred and looked up at him as the pain bit into her. Her lips trembled like a child's with pain and fear when she saw his bloody hand come from behind her back. He quickly caught her up under her arms, trying to avoid touching the worst of her ripped and torn back, totally disregarding the blood now seeping into his own jacket.

The stairs were too steep and too narrow to carry her with any degree of comfort.

"Steady on. You know the fireman's hold? OK. One, got it? Two, here goes. Three!" He swung her over his back, her head bobbing and her arms hanging limp. He went down the steps as quickly and cautiously as he could, holding her as steadily as his shaking arms would let him, urgent to find a place of safely for Ann.

"Mrs. Dray! Mrs. Dray! For God's sake, be useful, damn you! Where's the nearest hospital? I don't mean that cottage place, I mean a real hospital! Quickly!"

Mrs. Dray was predictably slow to come up with an answer.

"Come on! The hospital! Where is it!" He cursed himself for not having looked it up before they left to show her the house. He'd been too eager for her to see it. All pertinent information: schools, fire protection, nearest medical aid—all standard information for every agent. The blank for medical aid had been filled in with the name of the little cottage hospital, utterly useless now. In his anger, he gripped Ann harder than he needed. Ann woke up.

"Oh, please, I do want to buy the house. Please tell them!"

"My love, that is not the standard way to buy a house," he said very softly.

She didn't hear. She was out again. Shades of D'Oyly Carte.

Chapter 13

Damage Control

T hen he was faced with trying to make sense out of Mrs. Dray's garbled instructions for the way to Woodside Hospital. Finally, arduously, sign after sign, the sign for Woodside Hospital pointed the way with a bright red Emergency sign. Ann was in the right place and in the right hands. Mr. Herrick was suddenly superfluous.

Allen paced the waiting room for what seemed like hours, turning whenever someone came through the all-important door. Finally, a doctor came through looking as if he were hoping to find a Mr. Herrick.

"She's lost a lot of blood, as you know," the doctor said, eyeing Herrick's jacket. "But she's a plucky one, and she'll be all right in the long run. All surface stuff, but that's where the nerves are, of course. She'll be right tired of lying on her face for the time it'll take to heal. She's still in recovery, so you might have time to go out and buy some flowers or some such." This was common doctor language for "Please get out of our hair."

Herrick asked the receptionist where the nearest place to buy flowers would be and found out far more than he needed. The receptionist was a cheerful, helpful soul and obviously scented a romance.

Herrick walked out of the hospital in a daze. Ann was going to be all right! All that blood, and she was going to be all right! This from Herrick! His former fellow agents, not the house-selling ones, would have howled. Romance? They would have howled still more. Was he, Herrick, howling? Well, was he? No.

Where had she said that flower shop was?

The receptionist's directions were infinitely more accurate than those Mrs. Dray had been able to dredge up. Given her position and profession, the receptionist probably had been asked for those directions far more often. Now Herrick was introduced to the arcane language of flowers and their meanings between a man and a woman. The more fool he, to think real estate language was esoteric!

There is a whole language of the meaning of each flower, did he know? Love-in-a-mist. Yes, he knew. Just how close a relationship was it? Did he wish it to be more close or less close? Was she young? What color were her eyes? Closed, when he had last seen them, but he couldn't tell the sweet young thing behind the counter that.

Then he remembered her face when she had first seen the house. "Blue, or maybe turquoise." Allen had to admit that, yes, he was very fond of her.

"Proposal fond or just relationship fond?"

The options seemed to him to be very open. Again, he couldn't say "Well, she loves the house I love." Could he? He tried. That seemed to work. Price range? Well, what was the price range? From expensive to outrageous. Mildly expensive, he decided. Not flamboyant. Something to fit on a hospital table with all the other impedimenta hospital tables seemed to accumulate without spilling all the rest of them. Frankly, he didn't care how long the stems were, for Lord's sake. As if that mattered! Finally, he—or rather they—decided on a small bouquet of pink roses and pale blue somethings and some kind of light and very delicate fern, reminiscent of love-in-a-mist. Then came the hard part. The really hard part. What would the accompanying card say to the young lady? "Sincerely yours"? No. "Best wishes for a speedy recovery"? No. "We'll see each other when the lawyers have the papers ready"? Hardly. Finally, they settled with "Looking forward to seeing you soon. All is well with the house."

He had called the office to make her offer official, sometime during the weeks he had spent in the waiting room. Now, how to sign it? "Mr. Herrick" was all she knew. "Allen Herrick" was a pleasant balance between "Your fond agent" and "Mr. Herrick of Herrick, Makepeace, and Herrick Ltd."

Charles, his brother and the other Herrick in the firm, had seriously questioned her not considering a lower bid, at least at first. Allen replied that she was in no position to haggle and winced at his wording. Poor Ann! At least she would live! Allen had been appalled at how much that meant to him. Careful, Herrick. Yet already he knew they shared more than he had realized. Choosing flowers and the cards that had to accompany them could be very revealing.

Sir Arthur made a wonderful joke out of Ann's purchase of the old Thatcher house. "My dear, a house so poorly made that it tears you to pieces is thus so enticing that you buy it on the spot? For that ridiculous asking price! Oh, my dear! Ludicrous! I could have taught you so much about buying and selling! So very much! However, you never would listen, would you? That, I think, was the basis of our little parting of the ways. You simply never would listen. Discernment, my dear, the distinction of the well done from the not well done!"

He droned! He absolutely droned, damn him!

Ann had to listen to this on her stomach in the hospital bed. He had sent long-stemmed red roses, an even dozen with the longest stems Ann had ever seen on a rose. Wonderful! From her position on her stomach, one dozen straight, thornless,leafless green stems were all she could ever see. She longed for a big sturdy old-fashioned pencil-sharpener.

Chapter 14

Turbulence Along Converging Fronts

Mrs. Dray's rackety old Morris was to be seen and heard in back of High Place Old Lodge by the stable block. She had had the good luck of having caught Sir Arthur coming out the stables after looking over his new hunters and thoroughbreds and of cutting off his retreat. She had had the very bad luck of driving her dyspeptic old car too close to Sir Arthur's stable of hunters and thoroughbreds. Sir Arthur, in a towering rage, had pushed Mrs. Dray into the lodge through the gun room and into his private office at the back of the house. This very private room was dark, grim of atmosphere, and somehow more threatening than the gun room through which they had just passed.

Sir Arthur sat at a great distance, a very great distance, across the leather-topped mahogany desk carved to within an inch of its life. "I trust you have recognized fully the absolute folly of the following mistakes. One: you came here in daylight in full view of the entire staff. Two: you did this in a very public and noisy manner, calling all possible attention to yourself. Three: you drove that damnable nuisance, that flimsy excuse for a car, not only up to the lodge in daylight, you drove it right up to a stable full of very valuable and very highly strung horses. I can only hope that you realize the sheer stupidity of all these acts."

This was not the reception Mrs. Dray had expected. Still, she had great faith in the value to Sir Arthur of her news—her reports as she called them. She poured out her story without stopping, too involved in the telling to notice Sir Arthur's lack of response.

"Mrs. Dray"—he hoped to shut her up with this—"did you catch them in flagrante?"

"Beg pardon, sir?"

"Were they engaged in the act of sexual intercourse in your presence?"

Sir Arthur's bluntness came as a shock to Mrs. Dray, exactly as he had hoped.

"Well, not exactly, your lordship." She did not take hints well.

"Yes or no, Mrs. Dray?"

"No, your lordship."

"Did they embrace?"

"No, your lordship."

"Perhaps even kiss?"

"Well, he had his arms around her, catching her, like, what with her falling, my lord."

"However, no kissing?"

"Well, hardly, your lordship, what with all the sneezing and coughing and all."

"I believe I asked you to confine your answers to yes or no, Mrs. Dray."

Damn him! He'd suffer for this! Oh yes, he would! Two can play at this game! And he'd weasel me out of the pay he owes me! Mrs. Dray's own anger was rising—but too late.

"I am totally out of patience with you, Mrs. Dray, and do not intend to waste any more of my valuable time listening to your lubricious gossip. You may go." Sir Arthur rang for his very private secretary. By now, both were in a towering stage of rage, well noted by the very private secretary, who had been listening long before he heard Sir Arthur's ringing of the bell.

"No, my lord, but I'll tell you this for free, my lord! They laughed a lot!"

Sir Arthur was stunned! Stunned as he seldom had been stunned in all his experience in the—*the art*—of blackmail! He remembered his contacts in France, Germany, Greece, Turkey, Egypt, and Tunisia!

"They laughed a lot!"

Sir Arthur was suddenly close to tearing his hair out. Only its increasing scarcity stopped him. "How can you have the gall to think that—*that*—is any use to me! I'm better off without you!" He turned to the secretary. "Get her out of my sight before I commit mayhem! Get Henry and his crew to tow her and her execrable car off my property. Now! I'll not have my valuable horses disturbed by that rattletrap! Out! Now!"

Those who saw and those who heard from behind stable doors and from the high hay lofts made their own conclusions. Those who heard those conclusions at High Yews and in the Blue Boar that night came to further and even more colorful conclusions. The commotion did not last a week, and none of it mentioned Ann and Allen. Mrs. Dray, however, remembered. Her memory was the tenacious memory of the illiterate. In her mind, it built and built and became toweringly important to her life.

Chapter 15

Pleasant Weather Settling In

Ann gave much thought to the naming of her new house, but no name came to her. Dun-Dustin met with the reaction it deserved. Allen laughed and told her that she had writer's block. Ann retaliated by threatening to call her home *the Writer's Block*. Allen comforted her by saying, "It will come of its own sweet time." For both, it was a sweet time.

Mr. Herrick, in the interests of his client and the house his agency had sold her and partly out of guilt, totally unrealistic, over her injuries, was overseeing the refurbishing of the house. He preferred not to look further into his motives. The workmen liked him and respected his expertise and his appreciation of a job well done. They were quick to understand him when the job had not been done well. He had the reputation of his agency to uphold, after all. Allen was unwilling to think of Ann in a home shoddy in any way. He brought color samples and swatches to her in the hospital, knowing that thinking about a pleasant future was to best way to occupy her mind as she healed. The healing went quickly after that, and soon she was released. She relished that word. *Released!* Yes, a lovely word!

Mr. Herrick, Allen by now, sat back and enjoyed watching her slow, steady recuperation from those debilitating injuries. He found strong reliable country girls to dust and clean and take over the heavy work while Ann directed, instructed, and made hundreds of decisions. Allen, as a dealer in houses, homes, and domiciles, knew when all the auctions and house sales were going to be and whether they had anything to offer that could be of value to her. Sometimes he even drove her to them himself, finding them an excellent opportunity to watch people who did not know they were being watched. It was Allen who found a local man with a wagon and team who could transport Ann's new finds to her precious, growing, but still unnamed home. The locals called it the old Thatcher Place and would probably go on calling that for a few more generations at least. This, of course, only further frustrated Ann, but she took it out in her writing, which was flowing freshly now and becoming a greater and greater joy. Only rarely did she catch Allen's smile as he watched her so engrossed in her work. He was, as she had noted so much earlier, "coming along nicely."

Allen introduced Ann to the vicar and his wife and all the other people who would eventually make up her life at High Yews. Vicar Matthews and Amity, his wife, soon became friends of both Ann and Allen. Allen's life had taken on an entirely new facet, and he had been working with thrice-divided attention that was making him often distracted and weary. It also enlarged his hunting field, places where he could be seen without awkward questions arising. This turned out to be more productive than he had thought, making him still further active. However, he made time to see to it that Ann's newfound writing areas by the windows had broad tables and comfortable chairs. A typewriter (a new Remington), reams of paper, piles of exercise books, pens, and pencils. He found a new pencil sharpener, and he himself screwed it down to one of the sturdy old oak tables fast filling up with scattered sheets of paper. He bought her a new and larger wastepaper basket. She practiced making baskets with it to help cool her frustrations when a page did not turn out right no matter what ideas she put on it. At least she could still hit a basket.

The trips to the auctions became curiously significant to Allen as he heard bits and pieces of the information that made such an important part of his life—a part that Ann knew nothing about. For instance, he realized that Sir Arthur seemed to have lost his taste or his touch for tormenting all those little people, the small fry in the country around him. Allen's reports on Sir Arthur's activities—his nets of blackmail spread over the countryside and across the Channel—were reaching higher and higher levels of command. Even Allen's brother, Charles Herrick, had been caught for a while and had caused havoc for Herrick, Makepeace, and Herrick. Allen fulfilled his commission to report back to Scotland Yard everything relevant to Sir Arthur's nets and his catches. Some of his reports stayed with the Yard. Others were considered to be better dealt with under the auspices of the Foreign Office. All of them were important. Charles could not know Allen's second reason for his return to High Yews.

Chapter 16

Just Saved From Further Squalls

Ann was able to go back and forth from High Place Old Lodge to the new house, bringing the few things that had been really hers to help make her new house really hers as well. Being in High Place Old Lodge, the few times she went, were unnerving experiences. Where once she has been seen and not heard, now she was invisible. Arthur ignored her, and the word had trickled down by way of Braithwaite and Miss Tilly the housekeeper, that she was to be ignored unless she tried to take anything not legitimately hers. Since she was officially invisible, she was often in a position to hear things that would have been kept away from her ears before. The staff talked as if she were, in reality, not there at all. They knew she was no longer in a position to have them fired without a reference. She was as invisible on one side of the green baize door as she was on the other. The so important, so symbolic green baize door.

The last time Ann ventured back to the lodge, she overheard Mrs. Dray's harsh voice raised in Miss Tilly's parlor. "How you could think to dare!"

Yes, that was Mrs. Dray, all right, but who was the other?

"With your father scarcely in his grave!" Ann heard Miss Tilly's voice twittering like her canary in the background. Her canary made as much sense. Mrs. Dray, however, was easy to understand, every syllable, as always.

"How could you possibly think we would have any truck with the offspring of a common thief? In this honorable house? Off with you, and don't show your curly head here again! I warn you, Miss Fuzzy Top!"

Delusions of grandeur! Where in heaven's name had that *we* come from? Really, where? Interesting! Mrs. Dray was no longer employed by any Riddecoombe Ann was aware of.

Ann's thoughts were interrupted abruptly as a tall thin girl ran through the baize door and started them both running down the long corridor. Ann took one glance at the pale figure of Letice Hampton-Gray and rushed her across the great hall into the sunny conservatory.

"Good morning, Thompkins. Hope the knee is better!" Normalcy, normalcy. Always keep it sounding normal, whatever you said. "The sky is falling. Oh, really, and on a Wednesday too."

Ann waited briefly for his answer, rejoiced with him that the knee was indeed better, agreed with him that the coming warmer weather would be a blessing, and shoved Miss Hampton-Gray through the side door. "I warn you that her ladyship, Mrs. Dray, is on her high horse today, Thompkins. We're off! McKinzie might let you work on the far spinney today, if you asked him right. Just a hint. Can't waste the good weather, you know!" She smiled at the gardener's rejoinder as she pushed the other woman through the door.

Ann was not through with her captive, not by a long shot. She led the still-shaking young woman to her almost-new car that had been her first purchase with her freedom money. It was neat and smooth in its gears and a mossy gray green that was almost invisible along the country lanes. Ann had to drive carefully along those lanes just because the car was so inconspicuous that faster, brighter cars often mistook it for part of the scenery. Ann was developing a habit of being inconspicuous, something she was unconsciously picking up from Allen. It didn't occur to her until much later just how useful that could be.

"If anyone asks, just say I'm kidnapping you." Ann smiled quickly at her captive before she turned off the only lane that would eventually bring them to her new house. She was driving at her usual slow pace and trying to be as casual as possible, but questions were whirring around her mind like startled partridges. The only response she got was the sniffs and sobs that she had been hearing ever since they left the lodge. Maybe this was not such a good idea after all.

Ann stopped the car along the verge, reached into her glove compartment, and handed her a good-sized handkerchief. Then she reached farther into the compartment and took out a large torch. Opening the door, she stepped out and went slowly around the car, looking carefully at each of the tires with a calm but concentrated focus. She was sure that if anything had been destined to go wrong with the car on the drive home, it would have happened by now, but it gave Ann a small space of time to think, and Allen had been so insistent on this ritual. Finally, she got back in the driver's seat and leaned back, letting out a long breath.

Chapter 17

Escaping The Storm

A nn smiled as she realized she was a little weak in the knees herself. "I'm not used to taking care of myself, and cars are new to me, so I feel safer with a good looking over before we get to the steep parts."

"Where are you taking me?" Good Lord. Not "Where are we going?" but "Where are you taking me?"

"We are going to my new house. I am Lady Anne Riddecoombe. Please don't let that scare you," she said, since it seemed to have done just that. "I have separated from my—still hard to say it—from my husband and am living alone now. I am beginning to realize that I might be in danger doing this, and"—Ann laughed—"and I thought I was rescuing you!"

"You are! Never doubt you are! The lettuce girl was being eaten alive back there."

"I've heard slugs are the very devil with lettuce." Ann gently rested a hand on the "lettuce girl's shoulder. "May I ask who the lettuce girl is when she's at home?"

"I'm Letice Hampton-Gray, and I haven't got a home. Nor any friends nor anyplace to keep Van Eyck!"

Oh god, Oh god, Ann thought. *I couldn't have started out in a worse way!* "Would you like to be my guest for a while, until you can sort things out? You really would be safe there. Two are far safer than one, you know. I really mean this as an invitation. You could be a great help to me, really you could." Maybe being helpful would be more understandable than just being a guest.

"Oh, but I couldn't bring Van Eyck!"

"And Van Eyck is?" Besides a delusion.

"My Turkish Van cat."

"Ah. You mean the kind that swims!" This was not a great deal of information, but Ann considered it a start and was grateful for it. You had to admit it was better than a delusion.

"Right." Letice took a deep breath. "You know more than most. I got her when we were in Turkey last time, at the tell where my father was director for the season. The truth of the matter is that my father was the administrator of the Peabody Museum of Egyptian and Near Eastern Art. He was found, somehow, to have embezzled a great deal of money from the museum, and before it could be explained, he ran his car into an embankment. You've heard of the case?"

"Yes, a little, not much."

"It was all hushed up until the 'accident.' Then it was all over the press. They loved it. My brother came home from Scotland with his family and took over and sold everything, including my books. My fiancé decided I was no longer suitable, and Van Eyck and I were left homeless and with no support anywhere. I never expected to have to support myself, and I refused to marry the idiot my aunts tried to foist me on to. An actuarial accountant, if you would believe that! Now Van Eyck is at the shelter, and I'll lose her if I don't get her back soon." Tears threatened again.

"Are you allergic to dust?"

"No, but what—I mean, is that really, really important?"

"More important than you realize. Is Van Eyck allergic to dust?"

"No, but, again, what does this have to do with, well, with anything?"

"Will you be my guest and help me fight my dust until we can sort this out?"

"I'm the daughter of an embezzler! I think that might be more important than dust!"

"Are you also an accessory before or after the fact?"

"No! What do you think I am?"

"Just what I am trying to find out. I myself am a young woman recently separated from her—it is still hard to say—her husband. I recently had an accident while I was looking for a new and different home and am just out of hospital. I need a live-in assistant to help me get the house clean and refurbished. I thought I could do it all myself, be free and independent and all that. I've found out, to my intense shame, that I just cannot do it all alone. I need help with, well, with getting all the dust out of the place. I need curtains in the windows and food to be cooked and my complaints to be listened to. You would be more a paid companion than a servant. I do not need a servant! I do need someone to share the house with me. I also need to be very, very frank with you. My husband is Sir Arthur Riddecoombe."

Letice gasped.

"Yes, well, he seems to be my enemy as well. Mrs. Dray is another enemy we have in common. My house is that one up on the hill in front of us. I'd like just the two of us to go there and talk, just have tea and talk, and see if something can't be worked out that would suit us both very nicely. Something that would suit Van Eyck as well. Are you game?"

Letice, a little dazed, nodded.

"I really can't be having with *Letice* and with sobs and nodding. Can you be just Letty and let me be just Ann?"

Letice suddenly became Letty. "I would like that very much! Oh, thank you! You have no idea!"

"I have a clue. I lived with that man for almost three years. Tell me, does Sir Arthur have anything to do with the Peabody Museum?"

"He is a trustee. How did you know?"

"I smelled him."

Ann put the car in gear, and they finished the drive up the hill to the little mostly bare house.

They were in the kitchen, and Ann was busy putting the kettle on and wrapping Letty in a blanket and generally fussing.

"Shouldn't I be doing all this?" Letty asked timidly.

"Would you know how?" Ann answered bluntly.

"Well, no."

"Good. I value honesty. You will learn. As I said, you will be my companion and not my servant. I can teach you everything I will expect of you, and I will share all the work. What I don't know about keeping a house, we will learn together. In exchange, you will tolerate me when I am writing, and you will learn how hard that can be. Does this seem possible at all?"

"Oh, yes!" Letty was truly attractive when she smiled with huge blue eyes that seemed somehow to go out of focus occasionally, and blond, naturally blond hair that waved, also naturally. Everything about Letty seemed uncontrived, unsophisticated, but very real. That warm heart was also very real, Ann was to find, to her continued, and very real, comfort.

"Excellent!" Ann was enjoying herself. Maybe this would work out after all. "Now do you have the phone of the shelter where Van Eyck is currently residing?"

Letty fumbled through her bag and handed Ann a small card.

Ann took it, saying, "I did say you will be safe here. I offer this as the estranged wife of a man I consider extremely dangerous—for what that's worth. However, I do have friends, and this has every possibility of working out very well. We won't know until we try. I'm willing, very willing, in fact. Are you?"

"More than I had ever hoped!" Tears stayed wherever tears live normally, and a small smile appeared.

Ann walked into the hall and could be saying things like "Yes" and "Good home" and "Tomorrow, then. Thank you very much. Yes, I understand. You did say a good watch dog, didn't you? Excellent!"

"Watch dog?" Letty ran into the hall! "Watch dog! No! You misunderstood completely! Oh, how could you!" The tears threatened to break out again.

Ann leaned against the wall helpless with laughter. "Two for the price of one! Do you know how sometimes animals, race horses and things, develop relationships with other animals in times of stress?

Race horses have a cat or a goat that they simply must have to live with, or they won't race at all? Well, Van Eyck and a little schipperke, that's a little black dog, have developed this weird kind of relationship, and the good people at the shelter are in a pother about having to separate them. So I said I'd take them both—on probation—the dog, on probation. Van Eyck is yours. Are you willing to give it a try? For their sakes? It would be a shame to separate them when they are such good friends and can support each other through these hard times!" Ann tilted her head as she always did when thinking hard and trying to be convincing. She was talking about the dog and the cat, of course. Of course she was.

Letty had given up trying to keep up with Ann. "Of course."

"Now, what will we need? Leashes, bowls, rugs to sleep on, or does Van Eyck sleep with you on the bed?"

Letty nodded shyly. No one had ever let that happen before. Not that it had never happened before, just that no one had ever known and still let it happen.

"Food," Ann continued, "and . . . What else? Do you know a good pet supply store? Where did you use to go? Oh, the servants, yes, well, we are the servants now, each of us. I'll do the dog. I'm used to dogs from the farm. Oh, there is so much to talk about! You can take care of Van Eyck."

Letty noticed that Ann never called her the cat. It was always Van Eyck, as if her name was due her.

"There is a general store at Oakhill, that might be the best place to start."

Ann picked up the phone directory again. "Yes, can you tell me what supplies you carry for a small"—Ann looked at Letty, who nodded—"for a small cat and a medium-sized dog? Well, just about everything, really. We're adopting, you see. Yes. Thank you, we'll be right there. Yes, I know it's late, but we're not far. Thank you. Oh, it's

Lady Anne Riddecoombe. Yes, that's right. Oh, you're very kind! Yes, thank you so very much!

"I think this could be fun," Ann said, more to let Letty hear the word *fun* and keep it in her mind. "Sometimes, once in a blue moon, the title is useful. Don't you know?"

They left without checking the tires. Fortunately, they had left before the shady dim shadows that were moving up through the back pastures came to the top of the hill.

"We'll pick up the animals tomorrow morning," Ann explained as they parked in front of the general store on High Street. "Paperwork, always paperwork. Oh, they mentioned shots. Van Eyck has had all her shots? Of course, she couldn't get into the country without them. Good! Then the paperwork will all be ready in the morning, but this afternoon would have taken too long."

Soon they were busy collecting the absolute necessities for dog and cat. No, they did not need the ribbons or rhinestones on the leash. Yes, they wanted a collar that would fit a size-medium dog, Ann assumed. Letty was picking out a smaller collar for Van Eyck, simple but elegant, and on sale. Food there was in quantity, if not exactly the quality Van Eyck was accustomed to. Shelters did not cater to the needs of spoiled cats either. Van Eyck would have to become accustomed to it or share the dog's food—a likely scene at best. Was Van Eyck strictly an indoor cat? They would just have to work something out. A box, yes, of course, what did they have that would suit a small cat? So many kinds of, what was it? Litter? Ah yes, the servants. Why had she not guessed? Finally, they were content with the pile of absolute necessities they had accumulated on the counter, paid, thanked, and were thanked and thanked again and hurried back out to fit their new purchases into the little car.

In a whirlwind of Ann and Letty, they drove back up the lane and up the hill to their new home. They emptied the car of all the absolute necessities, plus some minor purchases to make a supper with, and, locking all the doors, collapsed, one on the sofa and one the only chair, breathless.

"Do you always go at this pace?" Letty asked her new friend.

"Only when absolutely necessary," replied Ann, absolutely believing it.

The two shadows moved toward the little car. The muffled sounds were not heard by either Ann or Letty, fast asleep in their new home. Only one other heard, in the quiet shadow under the trees by the side of the house. The night became deeper and darker until much later, when the thin moon rose. Only the common night shadows to be expected this time of the year in the ordinary cycle of life in the countryside darkened the land close to the little house.

Chapter 18

Roads May Be Dangerous

Allen came on an exceptionally early visit the next morning. Ann had not been expecting him quite this early, but she knew that his "viewing" schedules had to accommodate the working man who needed a home as well as the more idle rich who wanted yet another home. Ann let Allen in after going through the series of taps and counter-taps he had devised and she had memorized to please him.

She smiled her just-for-Allen smile, and he smiled back in his—as she would come to know it—just-for-Ann smile. It was quiet for a bit while Letty studied the glorious view from one of the front windows and came to her own conclusions. Then Ann remembered where they were and who had been added. "Allen, this is Letty who is staying with me for a while. She has had something of a disaster in her flat and is coming to help me with my battle of the dark lords of the dust."

"Perhaps, possibly to distract you while her friends poke nails in your tires." Allen suddenly sounded not like Allen at all. Nor did he look like Allen at all.

"Allen, what? What are you talking about? I checked the tires yesterday!"

"Then last night while you two were sleeping—or one of you was—your tires were studded with just enough nails to get you to that curve at the bottom of the hill. Where you would be going quite a clip as you went off the road and down the embankment into the river."

"Oh, Allen, *no!*"

Allen took Ann roughly by her arm—her suddenly still painful arm—and led her out to her car. Looking back at Letty, he said, "You will please stay where you are until we can find an explanation for this, my sudden stranger."

Ann still could not take this all in. Allen so very strange! He was the stranger, not Letty. Then she saw what he was forcing her to kneel and see. Nails. Many, many nails. All halfway driven into each of the four tires. It would have been over-kill if the pun had not been so painful. Ann was stunned.

"Letty, Letty, come and see! Remember yesterday when I went around the car with the torch and looked so hard at all the tires? I thought it was all, well, too serious." She looked somberly at Allen. "It wasn't, was it?"

Letty stood ice white in the doorway. "All what was too serious? Ann, what has happened? What is it?"

"Nails, nails driven into the tires, all of them. We would have gone over the rail and down . . ." She couldn't finish.

"So that when we ..." Letty could imagine what might have happened as well as Ann and Allen could. "Oh god!"

Allen helped Ann up, and she leaned on his shoulder. Not, he noticed with pleasure, on the car. "Allen, you've been right all along, haven't you? There is danger! Real danger! I don't understand, Allen. Why to me? Hasn't he done enough to me?"

"He has done too damn much to you. Are you sure it was Riddecoombe or his buddies? Who else, Ann? Think! What other enemies? Were you really going to go out together this morning? Was Miss H-Gray possibly going to have a sudden headache?"

"No! No! We were going back to pick up Van Eyck, her cat, at the shelter. Van Eyck who painted would be at a museum, not a shelter." A poor attempt. A very poor attempt. Something had to take the ice out of the air! If it meant Ann had to play the clown, so be it.

"Letty's cat, a Turkish Van, and the nameless one, the schipperke who was—who is going to be our watchdog! We were going, both of us, that was the point."

"Forgive me, Miss H-Gray, I may have been hasty. This has not been a single isolated incident. It still comes down to motive. Ann, for God's sake, think! Who! Who would do such a thing and why."

"Police. No, I don't mean the police did it. I mean we should call the police."

"Ann, your lines are cut. Please." Allen was his gray-stone controlled self but he was desperate for her to understand him underneath that control. "Please! Can you see now how important this is! Ann, you write. You told me you write for pleasure. This time, write for your life! Sit down and think of all the connections you have with everybody you know. How long have you known them? When did you last see them? What was the atmosphere like? Is this someone who might want to get to Sir Arthur through you? Does someone want to blame this on Sir Arthur for revenge? Do you realize how deep Sir Arthur is in things that make revenge so easy to think of when you think of him? Do you know any, any one of the people who come and go at High Place Old Lodge? What do you hear at the dinners he lets you attend? Anything and everything! Think and then get it down on paper! Promise?"

Ann didn't have time to stop then and wonder how he already knew so much about her life. That came later. First came the beginnings of the skein.

Allen had driven his "work" car, so there was plenty of room. They went to the police station at High Yews to report the vandalism and something more than vandalism.

Allen made several calls while Ann and Letty went through their day, step-by-step, in a daze. Their minds still not taking it all in.

The constable drove out to Ann's house and went over the ground thoroughly. Allen had already gone over the ground even more thoroughly. He explained why he had been there last night and why he had had reason for suspicion. Constable Stites had merely laughed and mentioned something to the tune of "Boys will be boys!" and driven off. Allen watched him drive off, frowning thoughtfully.

Allen also drove off, but only after promising to be back as quickly as he could and making them promise to stay inside and out of the way of "that ignoramus!" Ann and Letty had no problem understanding his meaning. They could easily guess at the adjectives with which he embellished it as he drove down the hill.

About an hour later, two cars drove up to the house. Allen's had come in a long second. The first car had been driven by a middle-aged man of military bearing, tall, broad-shouldered, with red hair graying at the temples. The military mustache was still as red as Ann's hair. His eyes were very light gray, except when he frowned. Then they turned dark from the shadow of luxurious eyebrows.

"Ann, Letty, this is Major Alex Atherton. Major, this is Lady Anne Riddecoombe and Miss Letty Hampton-Gray."

"My, you do run in notorious company, Herrick. Ignore an old man. I'm pleased to make your acquaintance, Miss Hampton-Gray. I did not recognize you, Lady Riddecoombe. You may take that as a compliment."

Ann smiled, deciding to like the major.

The major bent down four times at the four tires. Each time he grunted and made a "tsch!" sound, which seemed to indicate severe displeasure, and shook his head.

"This means attempted murder, you're saying?" The major stood and brushed off his hands briskly.

"Exactly what I'm saying."

"You're also saying possibly related to the museum embezzlement case or to Sir Arthur?"

"And or or, yes. Unless it's something I have absolutely no handle on whatsoever, which frankly frustrates the hell out of me!"

"Scotland Yard."

"Would be the best bet, yes. Under the circs. as you say."

"What was that idiot of a constable thinking anyway?"

"Very little, if at all. The truth is that fact may fit in with some other findings. He did say he'd get the phone lines fixed. No mention of fingerprinting the box."

Allen talked with the major quietly. Ann had heard snatches of this and that. It obviously made serious sense to the two men, but not to her. Except that Mrs. Dray was mentioned once or twice.

72

After much serious discussion, the two men agreed that Scotland Yard needed to be brought in and as quickly as could be managed. This meant several calls from High Yews since Ann's phone lines were still cut.

Letty looked at Ann, who looked at Allen. He knew what was on her mind. "Could we stop by the shelter on the way back or sometime very soon? Ann did promise the shelter that they would be by to pick up Letty's cat and Ann's new watchdog this . . . well, today. Letty's especially anxious about Van Eyck, and I'd like to see Ann with a watchdog out there as soon as possible."

"Watchdog, eh? Good idea under the circs. I've got my Range Rover, why don't I bring them along? Ladies, if you'll join me?"

Major Atherton took some getting used to, but Ann and Letty were both glad to have him with them. They had no idea what an important man he would be in their lives. For now, they just knew they felt safer with him.

Chapter 19

Veritable Cats And Dogs

The major took immediate command of the shelter project. Once there, he took charge of the paperwork with the impressed and slightly overwhelmed staff. Nothing could come between Letty and the particular mew of a Turkish Van that everyone heard the minute the three came in the door. Letty ran to the Van's cage and gave Van Eyck her freedom. One of the staff rushed over and helped Letty put the little cat in one of the clever origami-like boxes they used to carry animals to and from the shelter. Letty added the towel she had brought, and together, with much mewing and cooing, the two of them reconnected, and all was well once more. For them, for now, at least.

The dog—really a puppy by the size of his feet—was another matter. He did not like his box. He did not like being put into it. Most of all, he did not like strangers. This was an excellent thing in a watchdog. The problem came when Major Atherton's peremptory commands did not impress him. Yes, he was a fine dog, an excellent dog, and yes, he would have to be trained to respond to Ann's voice and Ann's voice only—as soon as possible. Someone on the staff recommended a good trainer. Allen would arrange for a security check on the man as soon as possible. He'd been in the armed forces—it should be easy enough. The people who ran the shelter looked at each other uneasily.

"What do you call him anyway, don't you know? What I mean is, what are you going to call him? What should I put in the little box here, for the records, don't you know?"

"I call him Vanguard," returned Ann off the top of her head.

"Hah! Clever, what, for a guard dog, eh?" The major approved.

"Well, off we go!"

"Wait! We need to pay!" said Letty, trying to cuddle a box.

"Nonsense, all been done. My welcome gift to you both, don't you know!"

"Thank you so very much!" breathed Ann, trying to get Vanguard securely collared and leashed and into his box. "We appreciate your kindness in so many ways!"

Ann had decided that Major Atherton was a dear. A very influential dear. She desperately needed to talk to someone just like him, and soon.

"Soon" was not to be in the car. They were all thankful for the ingenious and sturdy origami boxes. Now if they could only have made them soundproof!

Major Atherton did all the talking on the way back to the house. His conversation was a mix of very complete information about the village and the people, interspersed with not very subtle questions about Ann and Letty. Who were they? Why turn up here? Where had they turned up from? The major was intrigued by Ann's mid-Atlantic accent. "Different perspective, eh? How do you find us? Acceptable, eh? Hope you will be happy with us."

By the time they reached the little house on the hill, Ann and Letty were both comfortable with the major and he with them.

Allen was already there, carefully studying the area around the car, being careful to keep on what gravel was left on the drive. Being professional. It occurred to Ann that while the trip to High Yews had been of the utmost importance because of the need to contact the highest possible sources in Scotland Yard, the major had been with them the whole time. What did that tell Ann about Mr. Herrick? What should she be learning about Mr. Herrick? About Allen?

"Well, Herrick, what do you think?"

"Hard to tell, sir. Two of them, at least."

"How can you tell?

"I was there."

That brought the major up short. "Were, were you? Just how was that, pray? And why did you not think to bring that to the attention of that wretch of a constable over there?"

Allen smiled wryly. "Would you be responsible for my bail, sir? Ann has been in danger ever since she left Riddecoombe, sir, if not before. At least when Sir Arthur thought he had complete control over her, he was fairly content. With the rift out in the open, his ego is what makes him a danger." Allen looked grim. "Major, I'm afraid it will be a long time before Ann is really free of him. She knows something she doesn't realize she knows or has seen someone who thinks she recognized him. Damn, I don't know!"

"Like that is it?" The major frowned. His eyes were a very dark gray.

"Oh, it's not passion. It's possession. He cannot bear to have anything taken away from him. It was the same way with the family place, High Place. You remember that mess, sir."

"Right you are! Very tricky, not to say dangerous, that was for a while there. You've been in this part of the country for a while now. Do you seriously think what he can't have, he'll try to destroy—again?"

"You remember the barn burnings, sir. Remember the dogs?"

"Yes, well." The major looked over at Vanguard playing with Van Eyck in the tall grass.

"Exactly," Allen replied, as if the major had completed the thought. "I seriously think this will be even worse."

Ann had been listening quietly.

"Please listen to me! In High Yews, Mrs. Dray is every bit as dangerous as Sir Arthur. She is far more connected with the local people, has far more power over them. I've been writing. Allen, you know my writing. My focus has been my life at High Place Old Lodge—about what I have seen there. Please believe me! I am afraid to keep on writing! What I am saying about both Sir Arthur and Mrs. Dray is hideous—out of a nightmare! It could be both damning and dangerous if it got out! I know Sir Arthur is the most obvious answer, but do not underestimate Mrs. Dray! Particularly when it comes to the local people! She has the power, not of witchcraft, as some in High Yews and the cottages really do think, but of blackmail and vandalism and sheer destruction! They are terrified of her, and rightly so! I see nails in tires as far and away more likely to be the work of those in Mrs. Dray's influence! Please, Major, could you please take the pages I've written so far and read them! I would feel so very much safer if you knew what I know! I know you are far more in the picture than I, but as Allen says, I may have seen something that I have no idea how to interpret! Please take what I have and let me know if I should stop writing about what I know and write about pussycats and little puppies with pointed ears romping in the grass! Are even they safe there? Are we?"

Allen and the major had simultaneous but not identical visions of Ann and Allen romping in the tall grass. Both decided the situation was far too serious to give voice to their reactions.

"I do see what you mean, I think, little lady, and while I don't think it is all that serious, I'd be honored if you would let me see what you have down. Hm, ah, yes. May I share this with Mr. Herrick, here?"

"Yes." Ann looked at Allen. Her eyes were huge with fear. "After all, he is the one who was here when the nails went into the tires."

Did that mean she didn't trust him? Why had this come up only when the major was here?

Ann answered his unasked question. "Yes, of course I trust you. I am also choosing to trust Letty. Nevertheless, if something did happen, what could you do? You were there that night, but the phone lines were still cut. Letty and I share a common background and the same enemies, I think. I know we do! Who are you, Mr. Herrick? Sometimes I think . . . I think you are the best friend I have. Sometimes I think you are the only friend I have. Sometimes I think I don't know who you are at all. That's when I think you don't want me to know who you are. That frightens me, Allen. You cannot know how much that frightens me!"

"Er, yes, Hum. Ah, I think I can vouch for Mr. Herrick, don't you know. I can give you that much."

"Ann!" Allen couldn't think of anything to say but "Ann!" He wanted desperately to comfort her, but anything he could say would only bring her deeper into the danger surrounding her already. He would comfort her later, more privately. He needed her comfort as well. But not with the major looking on. What he wanted with Ann was private, he realized, very private and shared and together. Always together.

Then he shook himself, looked at the major, and started out as far as he dared to go.

"I was in the war. You know that."

She nodded. The major, looking absently at the trees by the side of the road, also nodded slightly.

"I worked with several secret service units, some more secret than others, who worked against the Nazi effort to confiscate fine art from occupied France."

He paused. The major gave no sign of stopping him.

"I also worked with units who were after people supposedly on our side who trafficked in stolen arms, black market, and blackmail." There he stopped. That was enough for now. "I would not be telling you even this"—*even* this?—"except I can see you writing, and I can tell where your writing is going. This was, and still is, all of it, top secret. It was, and still is, extremely dangerous to know even that these groups existed. Do you understand? I am putting you in even more danger than you were. I'm doing this partly to keep you safer than you were, if that makes any sense at all. I desperately want you to understand the danger you are in. You are in deep waters, Ann, and dangerous things live there. You are dangerously close to them. Their disguises are many and very, very convincing. You know me, and you know the major. You know Nurse Appleby. We've run searches on the vicar and his wife. They could be, well, they could be godsends. We'll clear Letty as quickly as we can. I promise! Trust no one else, Ann! I mean it!"

A racing Vanguard chose that moment to run helter-skelter around the bushes and into Ann's legs. She fell to her knees and hugged the puppy, partly out of sheer relief and partly to hide her tears.

Over her head, the two men solemnly nodded to each other and turned to watch the puppy, his paws flapping in sheer puppy joy, chasing a carefree cat up the hill.

That evening, after a relaxed and casual supper, the major closed the door to the Range Rover and headed down the hill. He should have checked his tires, but he had a major's luck and was safe. That did not necessarily mean that he was not seen.

Chapter 20

Dirty Weather Coming In

Gil was dirty, hungry, exhausted, and terrified. He had been through the hell that was war in a concentration camp. He had been captured by the Nazis in a British uniform with a German accent on his tongue. They had not made it easy for him. Now, back in England, he was trying to fit back into a country that his parents had fled to after the last war. He was trying to find a home where no home may exist. He was different. Dear God, he was different! No one would trust him even after all he had suffered to keep true to his adopted country. As the very last resort, he was back at the little house on the hill. He knew the old man was gone. He knew the house was owned by one woman who lived only with one other woman—complete strangers. He knew it was hopeless.

He stood before Ann in the front doorway of her little unnamed house. "Please"—he winced to hear his parents' German voices in his own—"please, there is work here to be done? Is this not so? I have done it before and can do it again."

"You are Gil." It was a statement.

"Yes, ma'am, I am Gil. I know how to work. Work, I am not afraid of."

No, he was not afraid of work. There were many, many things he was afraid of, had been afraid of, but work was not among them.

"Do you know that Mr. Thatcher left you this barn and the little apartment you have made in it?"

"Please, what do you tell me?"

"In his will, his last will and testament. You own the barn now, Gil."

His face lit up like a child's in the reflection of the lights on a Christmas tree. "Left—to me?" Do you mean I own it?"

Ann smiled. "Yes. It belongs to you." The deed is with Mr. Thatcher's lawyer in town.

"How can this be? Is this legal?"

"English law is far, far, beyond me, but yes, the will was proven, and you are a British citizen. The barn is now your property. Please, if you'd like to come in and"—she tried not to stare—"wash up a little and have some tea? Something to eat?" Definitely something to eat.

Gil could only stand and stare. Was this heaven, or was he trapped? Before the war, he had loved this place. He had put his heart—his heart, did he still have one?—into this garden. Now it was so tempting, so very tempting!

That meant trust. Again, he was terrified.

Ann could see his fear, but not what was causing it. "Would you rather I brought tea out here, and we could walk around the place a little and see just how much really does need to be done? The rest of your life, it could take." She had meant it to sound comforting.

Ann disappeared into the house. Gil could hear her talking to another woman. Telling her to call the police?

Ann and Letty came out the door again, this time with a tray and—and food!

"Gil, this is Letty Hampton-Gray. She's sharing the house with me. Letty, this is Gil Harkness who used to work in the garden and has come back, thank heaven, to help us with it! Let's sit by the old apple tree, OK? It is still there, believe it or not. But needing much care. So much needs care, we don't know where to start!"

Letty was not like Ann, in at least one way. Letty blushed beautifully.

They sat. The bench was wobbly. It needed care as well. So much needed care. Not least the young man before them, who was also wobbly and twitched, his eyes wide and staring.

He had that nervous walleyed look as if he were trying to see all the dangers at once. Gil was one of the ones Ann had bled for when she had been so unfairly safe at the farm in the States. Of course Ann was perfectly capable of bleeding for a dangerous wild animal if it had been as thoroughly tortured as this young man had been. He was lucky to be able to live in the world she saw about her and to react with any amount of normalcy.

Letty could see his shell shock as well. Who could not? Who would believe that such a large man could be so much like a frightened hare?

Allen could. "Just what do you think you are playing at?" All Allen's anger was boiling up over him, scalding like a cloud of steam!

Gil jumped back, shaking with fear. "Please! I am no threat! This used to be my home." He thought a moment.

Ann waited to see if he would come to the right conclusion.

He did.

"This is my home, if the young lady says true. I am Gil Harkness. I own"—here he turned to Ann, who nodded—one nod, a serious nod. "I own the barn and the little place to live in it, which I myself built. The loft. I have come home to work as I did before. As any returning soldier—British soldier returning to his home."

There! He had said it! His head lifted.

Ann grinned. She was clearly on his side. What need was there of sides? Wasn't that the whole point?

"It's quite all right. I am no threat to Gil." She had thought it clever, the transposition of their parts in this scene. In a flutter-headed way, perhaps. Perhaps too much of a joke than fitting, but with a purpose.

Both men seemed to have come to the conclusion that the words were far and away too flutter headed. At least they had agreed on something! If that were the price of peace, so be it!

Allen scowled, his face dark, forbidding. His peace was not so easily won. "All right, very good. Prove that you are Gilbert Harkness!"

Silently, Gil rolled up his right sleeve. There were the damning numbers. The numbers of a nonperson. Of a thing. Of a piece of Nazi property.

The silence held for a long time.

Then Allen took out a notebook and copied the numbers down.

"Oh, Allen, how could you!" Ann turned away.

Gil even held his arm out to the light so Allen could read the numbers more clearly.

Something in Ann died.

"That can be verified, of course."

"Of course." Gil was using the same level tone.

"You say you are returning here to work as Gil Harkness worked before the war. Just what was your business here?"

"His business here, Mr. Herrick, is to eat food and drink tea like a civilized person. You may fake it if you try hard enough. Then we, Gil and I, are going to work out a civilized agreement allowing him to work on *my* property and improve *his* property in the barn. Neither, I believe, demands *your* approval or even your presence. I am sure you have other jobs calling for your attention. Other innocent soldiers returning from Nazi prison camps for you to harass, perhaps. Is that another part of your former life that I don't want to hear about? And believe me, I do not want to hear about it! Good-bye, Mr. Herrick."

"Ann!"

"Good-bye, Mr. Herrick."

Ann turned angrily and, followed by a very reluctant Letty, went back to the kitchen with her head held high and took the hysterical tea kettle off the stove. With the calm of utter control, she continued to prepare tea for herself and for Letty and for Gil. Three cups. Only three.

The silence inside the kitchen drowned out the silence under the apple tree. Van Eyck came and begged for some cream. Vanguard came and whined at the door. Looking out the door as she let the puppy in, Ann stopped short. Carefully, she put her shaking teacup back down on the table. It still rattled and spilled.

To Ann's complete shock, she saw the two men still under the tree but talking. Not shouting, not fighting, but talking.

"Letty! Come and look! No, leave the cup on the table, just come. Quietly."

Together, the two women watched as the two men talked.

Eventually, both men got up and walked toward the kitchen door.

"May we please come in?" asked Mr. Herrick. "The tea smells good from out here."

Silently, Ann opened the door.

It seemed that the making of agreements and contracts was men's business, and had made them thirsty. As Ann poured fresh water into the kettle, Allen found some blank paper on Ann's writing table and, with her silent permission, began to draft a contract between Lady Anne Riddecoombe and Mr. Gilbert Harkness concerning the work required and the salary to be paid for such work. Such work to continue twelve months of the year until it was agreed by both parties that the said contract should become null and void by agreement of both parties.

Allen was good with such words. He drew two long lines for their signatures and two shorter ones for the date. Then there were two lines for Allen and Letty to sign as witnesses. All was done in complete silence. The pause was long as Ann read over the entire contract as carefully as her understanding of Allen's writing permitted.

Finally, the tea was ready, and biscuits were offered on one of Ann's treasured antique plates. Allen knew the plate signaled a tentative truce. They had found it at an auction together a month ago. He remembered that auction. He had found out much of interest about Mrs. Dray at that auction.

Ann strived to return to the old friendship she had cherished. She really tried. The plate, she thought, had been a start.

After Gil had gone over to the barn and Letty had tactfully gone up to her room to read, she said, the two of them were left in the comfortable kitchen by the fire they didn't really need, and silence fell again.

"His name isn't really Gil Harkness, you know."

"Oh, Allen, that is not the way!" She wept inside. "I gather there is more to come?"

"His real name is Gerhardt von Bingen—as in Hildegarde. He was born here of German parents who came over right after the first war. He seems relatively safe."

Ann finally exploded. Anger always brought out the American way of words with Ann. "Oh, Mr. Herrick, that just relieves my mind something fierce! Are you going to do an international search-and-find operation on every man who comes through my door? *My* door? Gil at least had the decency to knock first."

She dumped out the rest of her tea and began busily washing up the dishes and straightening the kitchen. The door opened and closed again. After a while of splashing and sniffing, Ann turned back to the fire to kick the embers back to life.

Allen was leaning on the kitchen table watching her. He had indeed closed the door. He had just neglected to go through it first. Ann squeaked and jumped, and, for reasons totally beyond her understanding, ran into his arms. She had absolutely no reason to expect them to open for her. It seemed like a miracle when they did.

"I'm a heel. You, Ann, are my love, and you are in such danger! It makes me wild sometimes. I swore after the peace had been signed that I would never love again. I am a heel and a fool, and every word of that is true. The honest truth is that you should be running the other way, my love. To safety, not to me." In spite of his words, he held her even closer. Ann burrowed her head in his shoulder a little, just a little further. Finally the word *danger* filtered through his shirtsleeve.

"Danger? Real danger? You don't mean just scandal, do you? Allen, please! Life-and-death danger, and for you too?"

Allen laughed shortly. "Oh yes, me too. Always me too. Goes with the territory. I wish it could not be so for you—not you! For good and all, you are in it too now. Your writing, your skein, shows you know much more than you think you know."

He was silent for a while, his eyes half-closed as he gazed into the fire, thinking. Unconsciously, he rocked her to and fro. She leaned into his shoulder, and they stayed very quietly rocking. Years from now they would look back and see patterns, patterns forming into habits, but right now, they were both in the middle of new feelings and new fears.

Chapter 21

The Skein

F inally, Allen straightened as if to go.

"Allen, please, not just yet. There is something going on, and it's not just us. It goes way beyond us too, but not far enough beyond. It may be—I don't know what. I just know. I feel it coming closer."

Allen nodded slowly, still staring at the fire. Coming to a conclusion. "All right, here it is. Almost full strength and all at once. Tea first, Ann? Let me make a pot of good strong tea with lots of honey."

She wrinkled her nose at this.

"Believe me you'll need it. Best thing for shock: strong tea with lots of honey. I'll talk while I'm making it." Allen got the mugs—her mug and his mug. Already they had their own special mugs. Then he put the kettle to the boil again. The homely actions seemed to help him think.

Ann watched the process, or the two processes—the thinking and the doing—together. *Dear God*, she thought, *let it be just like this in thirty years.*

Allen pulled up his chair and began. He saw the haunted look on Ann's face and smiled wryly. "We may yet survive."

Ann put her tea down and leaned forward, watching him intently.

"Much of this has been kept from you by the 'powers that be' because they don't know you as well as I do. It may be that few do?" He looked his question.

She smiled wearily and nodded.

He went on, "I know damn well for instance that your ass of a husband never caught on. Ann, we've go to do something about that, you know. You do know that as well as I do, but not now. Not yet. Let him continue to think of you as he has in the past. That will keep you hidden in plain sight. As you are."

She nodded meekly.

"I may trust in your retiring nature to keep quiet? As you say, if not you can fake it."

She winced. Ann had chosen a poor time to show Arthur her independent self. Arthur was more a snake in the grass, a viper, than an ass. Ann had simply, simplemindedly, been bored by him for a long time before she had learned to fear him. *Now there was a mask of exquisite devising*, she thought. Boredom. If Ann had not sought to relieve that boredom, made that choice to begin writing, and then had to begin the process of separation and looked for a place to be separate in because of the fear she saw in her writing when she put down the skein in all its dimensions, she would never have met Allen. How vast were the changes a very small stick can make in a very small stream.

"Ann, come back."

Obediently, she came back.

"Don't start thinking without knowing more of the facts. I'm having to go slowly here, trying to test just how far I can go without bringing down the powers that be like a nest of hornets around your precious ears.

"I'm on to something, and it's deep. It's very deep. The powers that be are several and sometimes not exactly on the same side all the time." He stared at her as if wanting to force her to understand. "The Riddecoombes are in it deeply too. Yes, Percival as well. Granted, he is the dimwitted younger brother. The weak may be venomous. Percy may be the maladroit—yes, I know it's another word for the gauche. It would be cute to say he's Arthur's left-hand man, but they can be as devious as, well, as rats."

"Yes," Ann said thoughtfully. "It may fit."

"May fit? What may fit, Ann! For God's sakes, don't be shy now!" His voice was sharp but filled with authority, frustration, and concern for her.

Ann began slowly, trying to echo Allen's usual objectivity and clear-sightedness. Realizing now how close to him she had become. How much he cared.

"The people who come and go. I write about the people who come and go. The ones who come to Arthur's parties. The ones who disappear." She paused to see if they were seeing the same things.

He nodded. The powers had lists.

"Well, their moods were often so utterly different before and after. The same people, you know, but so very different when they left. As if they had suddenly grown years older or had lost the most precious thing they had in their lives. Or had never realized how very bogus it had been all along."

This was painfully difficult. She was so very different herself from the Lady Riddecoombe who had watched those people come and go and change.

"How much detail do you want? Names, dates, before-and-after impressions?"

Allen had begun writing in his agent's folder.

"Allen Herrick, who in heaven's name are you?" Ann's voice was quiet but urgent. She couldn't keep the tremor out of it, the tremor or the love. Allen left his chair to kneel by hers.

"My love, don't be afraid of me. Please? I said we'd both survive, and I meant it. We will both survive—together. Can you trust me enough to tell me about your descriptions of the 'people who come and go'? That could help more than you know."

"Well"—long pause—"well, I had the windows measured for drapes, you know, a silly, flighty scheme such as women have. Arthur laughed, but it gave me an idea of how tall these men were. They were all men. One was about six feet tall, and all his movements were jerky, as if he were held together with rubber bands of different sizes, and some of the rubber bands were old and seemed as though they would break under one more strain."

"Sounds something like von Shlieman. Interesting. Go on."

"One was absolutely colorless, about five feet six inches or so—short for a man. He kept ducking his head, except it was all the ducking that caught your eye. If he'd walked slowly and quietly, I wouldn't have noticed him at all. He came in a big American car. I don't know the make, but recent. All the cars were dark, did I say? If I'd seen them all together, I'd have thought it was a funeral procession. Different makes from different countries?"

"Possible. Different companies or embassies. Strange they didn't change cars at some point along the way. Go on."

"Oh, there was the redhead. He always wore a hat, but his hair must have been very long, unruly, because it always stuck out all around over his collar. He walked, sort of bounced, like a clown who had been kicked out of the brotherhood and wanted to kick back somehow. It could have been a clown's outfit, a costume."

This time Allen laughed out loud. "Yes, I think I know the man. Please keep going!"

"There was one I really liked. He looked so very sad each time he left. Some of them just clammed up, no emotion at all. The redhead was furious. But this tall gray one, the one who walked so very carefully, as if he might break something, not on purpose, but by accident, and it would be terrible if he did—I liked him. Most of the others were just there. Some were slow, as if they couldn't believe what had happened. Others were furtive, as if they would go from bush to bush if there were any bushes. The redhead actually kicked at the gravel and then looked at the windows as if he were afraid he had been seen. I'd be afraid to smell his daisy."

Allen looked at her in sheer disbelief.

"In his lapel, you know, the way clowns have? Only daisies don't smell anyway, so it's all too silly!"

"Ann, do you have this down on paper?"

"Oh, yes. Of course. That is what writing is, Allen."

"Yes, but I mean as something we could show to Atherton? More than we talked about before?"

"Yes! Please, could we? I have carbons."

I'll give him a call now." Allen unfolded himself, Ann noticed. Did all tall men get up like that? She'd have to watch. She watched Allen.

Now she could hear his voice on the phone in the hall. "Yes. I think it could be a great help. You'd have to look at it yourself, of course. Scotland Yard should see it. Yes, it could be that important. I just don't know! Yes, I do have one of my feelings. Yes, we'll be here.

"He's coming over. Do you mind?"

"Mind! Allen, I am so very relieved. Even if it is nothing, it is something. Allen, can you understand at all?"

"I know what you mean, love. Has it been very scary knowing all this just by yourself?"

"You do understand! That is one of the real reasons I moved out of High Place Old Lodge! I was terrified someone would find it. I used the school paper that I was buying for the little school the Riddecoombes founded. Still, I was so very frightened—scared. The maids! And that Braithwaite! The maids call him Braithweight." Ann laughed, hoping that Allen wouldn't see she was crying too.

Allen smiled. "It won't always be this amusing. Do realize that."

Ann sobered immediately. "Idiot! I know. Believe me, I know! When some things are funny, even silly funny, you laugh when you can."

"Wise woman."

Chapter 22

The First Front Of Percival Approaching

Then Allen sobered too. "What do you know about Percival?"

Ann shuddered. "Enough to stay as far away from him as I can! He has all the malice of Arthur without the control. He is sometimes the more dangerous one because you can't predict how he thinks or what he'll do next. There is no logic there to follow. Fortunately, he is not there very often. Arthur hides him somewhere in Germany, I think. When he comes back, it is because he has made another mess of things that only Arthur can smooth over. Then there are many, many cars and many, many shadowy people in them."

"He's here again."

"Oh, Allen! No!"

"'Fraid so. Does he bother you here? When he's in the country?"

"Yes! He is just like Mrs. Dray, only as a malicious schoolboy. He drives me insane when I am trying to write!"

"Can't you just send him packing?"

"Yes, but you never know what he takes back to Arthur. You only know how he twists it then he tells it! Oh, Allen, now I am afraid!"

Just at that moment, the doorbell rang, and Allen went to let Major Atherton in. "Ann seems to have been doing some of our research for us, Major. I think you'll be interested."

Ann was carefully organizing her writing chronologically in a stack on the coffee table by her good reading light. The major seemed to be taking this all very seriously, although this could only mean making the "little woman" feel she was contributing something worthwhile.

As he read, he concentrated more and more on the descriptions Ann had recorded. At one point he stopped, reached inside his jacket pocket, and changed his impressive horn-rims for his more comfortable reading glasses. As he did so, he glanced briefly over to Allen. That wordless communication she had noticed earlier crackled through the air between them. Allen nodded.

Time passed. Then the major turned to Ann. "Young lady, do you happen to have carbons of these?"

"Of course. I hoped they might be useful. For something other than domestic accidents, I mean."

The major blinked but did not smile.

Allen remembered Ann saying "You laugh when you can."

"I would very much like to take all this with me and go over it at my leisure, if I may?"

Ann glanced at Allen. "Of course! I'd hoped you would! I'll get some paper, and we can wrap this up properly." She went back into the kitchen very quietly, hoping to overhear any comments. The comments were in a low undertone but sounded serious. Not just to please a "little woman" then.

"I'd be glad for your company and your comments, Herrick. Why don't you come along for a smoke and a drink while we think this one through. You've given us a great deal to think about, young woman. You have our sincere thanks."

Allen nodded. Turning to Ann, he said, again with this new seriousness, "Be sure to lock up when we go."

"Allen, it's still daylight."

"Lock up when we go! Give that monster hound free range as well. Has he been trained up enough that he's any good yet?"

As far as Ann could see, Vanguard was completely untrainable. That may have been why he had been in the shelter in the first place. He was good company though, when she felt as alone as she did now.

"Good-bye, Allen," she said in a small voice as she shot the bolts.

Percival. Percival was indeed back from wherever he had made his last mistakes and was taking it out on what he saw as the small folk of the village. He had always timed the incidents in his life with remarkable ineptitude. Tall, to the aggravation of his brother, but pale, narrow-eyed, he had what he thought was a sophisticated grin, but it came on his face as an inane leer. Ann despised him. He knew it, and he used it.

His catty remarks and close-to-obscene innuendoes were becoming more than Ann could take. He never came when Allen was there, but his topics of conversation were inevitably about when Allen had been there. He came in unasked, one day in the morning when she had stupidly left the door unbolted, and lounged in the most comfortable chair while she was writing just to see how much she could take. Letty escaped to the garden when she saw him coming.

Finally, Ann snapped. "Percy, I am not 'carrying on'! I am writing a small mystery novel, a small thing *but mine own*. The 'sudden blush' you strain your eyes to see comes from thrashing out a scene that has been giving me trouble, strangely ever since you came in the door. It may not be Marsh or Christie. It may not even be publishable, but it's mine, and I intend to see it finished. Now *leave me alone!*"

Percy needed just this. "Well, my dear, I'll leave you alone, but I doubt if Mr. Herrick will. Though I don't say I will at that. You are too much fun to play with. I warn you, Miss, or unfortunately for you, Lady Authoress, if Herrick continues his highly inappropriate attentions, I will draw these attentions to the attention of brother Arthur, and *he* will call in his hounds of war, or perhaps, more appropriately, his bloodhounds of blackmail. Knowing Arthur as I do, I can tell you his investment in loosening your leash will result in a divorce case all, I repeat, all in his favor. He invested in you to do just that and is just waiting on the interest to come in return. The interest, my dear, the *interest*. So amusing!"

On that vindictive note, he grinned, rose languidly from his—from *her* comfortable chair, and walked out of the house. Reveling in her mixture of fury, revulsion, and frustration—vindictive, adolescent, terrifying Percival.

He left Ann with the word *interest* ringing in her ears! Blackmail? Because of Allen's kindness and support? Was that to be the basis for divorce? No! She remembered that there had been times he had held her and comforted her, and it had been so wonderful! Could she turn to Allen now of all times? Could Percy twist what he had heard or seen into something as gross and revolting as a cause for blackmail? What had he heard or seen?

Chapter 23

Uncertain Weather Again

Lately, Allen had become withdrawn. Had it been just since she had given the major her writing? Was that all he wanted from her? All the respect, the trust, the love that she felt for Allen during those first furious months of writing when she had needed support. A stable, platonic, mature relationship? Possibly something more?

Something more for her but not for him? Had he gotten what he wanted, and was he now indifferent? She had to see Allen! What if Allen did not want to see her? That was the whole of it! What would she do without the suddenly irreplaceable Allen? Yes, Letty was a friend, but hardly a support!

Ann was panicking. All those evenings working side by side with the hot tea and the comfort of a companion who understood but did not interfere with her thinking as she worked. He never asked questions about her, her life, her problems. "Would tea sound good?" Yes. "Would you stand up in a court of divorce?" God! God! God!

"Ann, may I come in please? The door was unlocked."

Unlocked! She never kept the door unlocked. She had promised Allen!

Oh yes, Percival's unforgettable last parting lines. Ann had remained paralyzed in her chair from fear. Fear kept her there now.

"Please, Ann?"

"Yes, of course, Allen!" Slowly she got up and walked to the door. "Is . . . is Percy still out there?" Ann was whispering, being careful not to touch Allen while the door was still open. Percy, she remembered, had closed all the shutters when he had come in hours and hours ago.

Allen took Ann in his arms very, very gently, as if she were a child waking up from a nightmare.

"No, my love. Percy is long gone. I passed his supercharged toy at the bottom of the hill. He did not look pleased. Did he do something? Anything? Is there anything I can do? Talk to me, Ann. You are safe now. Really, really safe now. Here now." Slowly Allen brought Ann back to the kitchen of her own home with his arms around her. Home. Safe.

Except she was the one who was creating danger. Her danger and his danger.

"He talked about bloodhounds and blackmail and—and interest and Arthur taking me to divorce court and ruining our lives."

"Oh, Allen. I've asked you to help me so many times, and it has all seemed so natural, and now I don't know even if I had any right."

"Know this, Ann. I love you. Now, going from that, hopefully as a beginning, could you love me?"

Ann's knees buckled. Allen was delighted to have an excuse to hold her tighter. "Say yes or say no, Ann. You owe me that much."

"Of course I do! Would I be this frantic if I didn't? I just never thought to call it that. It just happened so naturally. Once I hear it, of course I know it's true! I can also hear what Arthur and Percival could make of it."

Allen made a great display of checking all the doors and all the windows.

"I really, really should be furious at you for leaving that door unlocked, you know. Didn't I tell you? Locks and bolts can save your life!"

"Yes, but it was the middle of the day, and he was in already."

"Locking the stable door after the horse was inside, I guess?"

"Something like that. Oh, Allen, please don't joke. He was so horrible! I had visions of judges in wigs and reporters and scandal and, and ruining your life!"

"On the basis of Arthur and Percival actually working together? Ann, it won't happen."

"Even if it meant money for both of them?"

Doubtful at best, my love."

Ann was furious with frustration. "You act as if this were nothing! I have been frantic for, well, forever, and you come in as if it were nothing and bawl me out for leaving the door open!"

"Ann, the threats aside, did he hurt you?"

"Threats aside! Threats to ruin your life? Yes! He hurt me! Allen Herrick, will you always be this impossible? He hurt me by threatening to hurt you. And that hurts like hell! Does that get through to you anywhere?"

Allen finished his thorough check of doors and windows. He pulled Ann to him.

He couldn't just tell her, but he could show her. Gradually, she became content in his arms. "Ann, I'm split into two or maybe even four elements here. Part of me sees my home as I have dreamed of it during the war—the image that kept me sane during those years. It was the image of a good thing, honest, trustworthy, worth the, well, all the horror, all the hell. I was fighting for the thing I would belong to when I finally made it back home. The things I love. You, for one, though I didn't know it at the time.

"The devil's in it that the various separate wars that each separate unit was fighting are some of them still going on. There are units fighting to return the fine, the lovely objets d'art that need to be returned to the people who should have them by rights. Some of them to prestigious museums, some to old families—some Jewish—that simply do not exist any more." Allen was silent for a while. "At any rate, each unit had to have the highest security possible, even the very small ones. This meant, when World War II was over, each separate war was not over for those units with lives of their own. With security units of their own.

"We have a peace, but we don't know what to do with it, how to live it. Some units have become blackmailers themselves. We know that happened here and, all too often, elsewhere. Spies are seldom spies for the fun of it, or even for the excitement. They are in it because they are blackmailed into it. The blackmail became a kind of recruiting process, horrible as that was. The ends, etc. The really dangerous ones, like the Riddecoombes, are the ones who are fascinated by the process of giving pain. There is the real horror. Worse luck, even now that horror is still protected by all this damned security that was originally put in place to protect us from all the Riddecoombes out there. It turned into a very, very vicious circle. How can we separate the healthy needed security that protects those working for a safe and sane England and the ones who work for themselves alone and for warped and sadistic purposes? The Riddecoombes and I both rely on security, but by god, for purposes as different as night and day!

"You, Ann, are part of what I fought for and what I am still fighting for. You are too damn close to these invisible front lines here in England itself!"

"No, Allen, I am in danger because I am too close to the Riddecoombes! My only safety lies in being close to you! He is the danger, and I will, Allen, I will help you fight the Riddecoombes and what they stand for. It will be the war effort I wanted so desperately to be a part of when I was in the States! All right, I am in the front lines without knowing it. Even without knowing it, I have been gathering information. I think even the little information I have found, and the major has much of that, can be vital if we fit it together with what you have already found. Doesn't that make sense?"

"All right, we start from what we are sure of. We love each other. Is that a given?"

"That is a given. Oh, Allen, is it safe for you to hold me?"

"I like it," he responded. After a while, he asked again, "Ann? Does this take us back to Percival?"

Ann was silent.

"Ann! Tell me!"

Yes, it takes us back to Percival. I am terrified of him!"

"Why? Could he blackmail you into betraying me?"

"Allen! Never! Never!"

"It has happened, you know. I've been too close, seen too many friends turn into deadly enemies. And die. Damn!" He had meant to keep it light.

Ann took it at full strength and more.

"My marriage to Arthur was wrong from the beginning. It should never have been. Here I was worried about being in a divorce court looking across at Arthur, and now I'm terrified of being in a morgue, looking . . . Oh, Allen! I love you so much!"

Ann, the strong, the independent, held on to Allen as if she could protect him from the whole world.

"It won't come to either, Ann. Honestly!"

"Percival or Arthur could either of them be right outside that door right now, with one of those fine shiny guns he has in that horrible room he takes people through when he wants to terrify them."

"I doubt it. Sergeant Bates would be in his way."

"I mean it, Allen!"

"So do I. Don't look, you're not supposed to know he's there."

Thunder rumbled, and Allen laughed.

"Seriously! Thunderstorms are my friends. My husband is my enemy. Our enemy. What power have I?"

"The power not to be afraid."

"Seriously. Stupidity can do the same."

"All right. Sorry to insult you, if this is an insult, but I think our Arthur is becoming tired of that game. If you were in the courtroom, he'd have to be there as well. In front of the same people. He is mostly ego. He had enough taunting from his associates when you were married. He hated it. Imagine how Percival would taunt him if he were to be divorced. Think of all the very true things you could say to a jury about Arthur."

"You didn't hear the things Percival said to me!"

"He said them to you. Not to Arthur. Nor would he ever say them to Arthur. Arthur would die before he let anyone know he was not in complete control. Yes, yes, I know the clever comments on Arthur's 'interest' building up. That was pure Percival, should such a thing exist. Also, remember—you have friends now. Far and away more friends than Arthur and Percival combined. What about the major? What about Amity and the vicar? Gil and Letty? Need I go on?"

"Yes. And what about Arthur's lawyers? Allen, he has false witnesses in his back pocket! Can you imagine a whole filing system organized by possible use of people he has some dirty secret over, just waiting to be useful to the man with such power over them, hoping for some trivial favor from him if they can be useful? Hoping not to die?"

"The point of this is that you have more real courage and more real moral strength and more real true friends than he has ever had or ever will."

"OK, so we're the good guys! One gun in the wrong guy's hand blows all that courage to smithereens."

"So we have Scotland Yard and sergeants guarding your door." He paused and thought until Ann could have screamed at him. After all, she thought, what else had she just been doing at him for the past hour? Bates should be getting an earful. She hoped it was Bates. A sergeant of some kind at least.

Finally, Allen said, "Yes, I think that would work. Let me start over and be quicker about it. I know things about Sir Arthur Riddecoombe and his precious Percy that, shown to any decent divorce lawyer in the country, would get you a divorce without any trouble at all. How's that?"

Ann continued to watch him intently. "You mean I've been going through absolute hell for weeks over this divorce thing, and all you can come up with is 'I can make all that just terribly easy, but I just can't tell you how'?"

"Remember our recent discussion about trust? Here is where it comes in. I have made a promise, a vow of honor if you will, to a very good friend from my old unit not to mention certain things until a certain time. Yes, I know that all sounds very high and 'jolly good, man' and all that, but damn it, he saved my life a few times! I for one am grateful for that.

"Right now, my primary interest is to set your mind at ease. I'll meet my friend—no, I can't tell you his name, but I'll get it through channels, as they say, and we'll reassess the situation. They actually say that too. This can be done. This will be done. I can't say any more than that this will happen! Trust?"

Ann closed her eyes, sighed, and held him very, very tightly—as if for the last time. He was back in the war again. Damn, love could hurt!

"I'll let you know as soon as I can get through the channels, promise. I'll let you know as much as I can, also promise."

Ann was trembling. "I hadn't realized a job selling houses was quite so dangerous."

"Oh, Ann, I love you so very much!"

"Only one more question." She stopped. Then "Am I a danger to you?"

Allen groaned. "Never, never think it, Ann. God!"

Ann held on tightly, drawing strength from him as he drew it from her—strength and love. Together and silent.

Thunder rumbled closer. Finally, it could not be ignored. Allen left by the front door after a brief conversation with the tall hydrangea by the step. The hydrangea saluted, and Allen went on to his car, took out his torch, and checked the Buick quickly and with professional thoroughness. Then he waved good-bye, knowing she'd still be watching, and left.

Chapter 24

Blood And Thunder

The storm was almost on top of them now. Ann went slowly around the house, checking the doors and windows, opening the first-floor windows just a crack at the top as she had been taught in the Midwest of the States, only there they would all be second-story windows—just to prove the world really was crazy—to balance the air pressure when the storm really hit. She'd never heard of a tornado in Wiltshire, but training once learned held. Then she set clusters of sturdy household candles in sturdy household candleholders and set them in shallow bowls of water around the tables. Finally, she made a sandwich and a strong hot mug of tea—in Allen's honor—and sat on the sofa in the writing room and settled down to watch the storm come in.

Ann had learned to enjoy a good storm in the Midwest. As long as tornadoes did not come with them along the squall lines that preceded the huge black billowing clouds with their stark-white anvil heads high above. You were safe from the storms as long as you were inside and hopefully below the ground line. Storm cellars were built before the houses were built over them. These cellars were used far more often for jams and preserves and the potatoes that gave them a musty smell, but you only really need that cellar once to have it earn its keep—by saving your life.

Ann had seen homes after a severe tornado had hit. There is really no such thing as a mild tornado. You learned that too. One house was split straight down the center. One half with the bathtub was still standing on the first floor. Only the plumbing held it up. The sink in the kitchen on the ground floor just beneath it was still standing as well. The stove and the WC—the things that had been within feet of them before the tornado hit were simply gone. Not twisted as in the holes left by the bombs of the London Blitz. Just gone.

Ann burrowed deeper into the pillows and tried to pretend they were Allen.

Outside, a shutter banged against the barn wall. Ann jumped. Now that Gil was really and truly hired, he should have kept the shutters well latched and the barn well locked. Serious damage could be done. Someone could be seriously hurt.

Chapter 25

Serious Damage

“**L**ady Anne, Lady Anne! You must here *commen*! Oh. *Bitte, bitte!*”

Ann woke up with a start. “Oh, please!” Gil had been told a hundred times. No more Lady!

Then she really woke up. She was still on the comfortable sofa in the library. She was still in her clothes of last night. What was Gil on about? It had to be something, the way his German kept interfering with his English. Outside, everything was awash. The rain had come down hard and furiously long enough to polish the mud until it shone, eye hurting, in the low morning sun.

“Gil! Here I am. What is it?” Ann opened the door, unlatching all the latches she had so painstakingly done up the night before.

Gil was frantic.

“Can't you just tell me? Gil, it's sopping out there!”

"*Du* must here *commen!*"

"All right, all right! Wait until I get my galoshes on! Now, what?"

The "what" was the huddled body of Sir Arthur Riddecoombe.

At least those were his clothes, his boots, and his blood. His blood. Diluted by the torrential rain, it was macabre in its dainty pink, almost feminine, effect around the dark rain-soaked body.

Ann's view became very dark around the edges for a moment. She clung to the shutter with just enough focus to realize that it was securely fastened down to the barn wall.

It was the shotgun she had heard. The shotgun that had taken off the head of the late Sir Arthur Riddecoombe. Shotguns are seldom neat guns. The job they did was thorough—often, as in this case fatal, but seldom neat.

Ann put her head between her knees on the soggy old bench by the barn. "Gil, call the constable, the major, and a doctor, and Allen. Can you remember those names?"

No. Too much like war.

Too right, too much like war!

The order would just have to change.

Police first. Always police first.

"Constable Stites, please! Oh, well, where can you find him? Oh. Well, when he does show up, tell him there has been a murder at the hill house. No! No! Not the old lodge. The little hill house. Tell him I think it's Sir Arthur.

Because his head has been shot off, that's why!"

"God, Allen, please be home, please! Allen! Thank God! Please, please, please come! It's Sir Arthur!"

"Sir Arthur? There? Ann what is he doing there at six in the morning?"

"He's been lying in the stable yard all night. Allen, he's been shot through the head with a shotgun."

Ann had to sit down again.

"Yes, I'm still here, just a little lower. Yes, I'm fine! Just, just—come!"

Tea. That was hot tea. She could smell it, and she could taste it, and it was very, very hot.

"Ouch! Oh, that's hot!" Damn it, Allen, what are you trying to do to me?"

"She'll do." That was Dr. Coates

"Welcome back, Lady Riddecoombe."

That was a warning.

"Thanks." Thanks for the warning.

"Enough honey?" Allen asked. Sweetly, he asked. Damn him again.

Ann realized that she'd been carried back into the library and wrapped in a million warm blankets. No, three warm blankets and the million cats Letty and Van Eyck had adopted. She felt no need to move. Peace. Allen. Her tongue burned, but she was content.

"So Gil found him about six this morning?"

"Yes, sir, I found him there when I came out of the stable."

"And then?"

"I called the lady."

"And?"

"She called the constable, only he was not there, so she called Mr. Herrick, and then she fainted."

The major turned to Ann. The major! Thank goodness!

"Have you any idea when this might have happened?"

Ann was aware enough to realize that the "this" meant the shooting, not the fainting.

"Yes, I think. I know I heard what I thought was a shutter bang against the barn when the wind just started. I remember thinking I needed to talk to Gil about being sure things were battened down before a storm like that. It can do a lot of damage."

"It did," the major replied dryly.

"Where was the sergeant?" asked Ann, remembering the hydrangea.

"Knocked out and tied up."

"Behind the big bush by the front door, I remember, you said."

"Never, never plant a big bush right next to a front door—any door!"

"I'll remember the next time I plant a big bush. The next time I can stand up."

"You know what I meant. I'm surprised Mr. Herrick, helpful as he has been in other ways, had not thought of that one."

"God, don't remind me."

"God, I wish I didn't have to. Time we got this whole thing coordinated, don't you know?"

"Ann." Herrick looked as haggard as she had ever seen him.

"Have some tea. It's still hot and there's lots of honey. You just need to stir it up, if you can." She smiled up at him, willing him to stop looking so very gray. He sat by her side on the sofa, trying to smile reassuringly. Instead he shook. Ann adjusted the blankets and cats so she could be closer to him to share body warmth. Allen was not generating any of his own.

"Any physical contact will be disregarded under the circs.," the major growled. "Just keep clear of the kitchen. Mrs. D's with us, along with—and I mean along with—Constable Stites."

Chapter 26

Clearing Skies

Then Ann realized.

She was a widow!

She was free!

Separate indeed.

She realized why she had felt so very different!

She realized so many things!

It took all the cats and the blankets and the sudden steel-like control in Allen's eyes as they looked into hers to keep her from shouting for joy! Allen was right though. Control was absolutely necessary, but control that was not evident control.

"Amity" she said, almost hesitantly. "Amity? Could she come?"

"An excellent choice, Lady Riddecoombe. Mrs. Matthews, yes! The very thing! I'll call the vicarage."

Even with Amity at her side, Ann had a long hard road to some kind of normality.

The hardest problem was her relationship with Allen. Now that what they both wanted so much was possible, it seemed impossible. Of course, the relationship was the same, strong and true. It reminded Ann of Allen's tea—strong and true and very, very sweet. It was also very, very warm. When they were alone, it was good, it was wonderful. But they were so seldom alone. Everyone seemed to want to comfort Ann, either that or to congratulate her. Letty was another great source of strength because she knew the truth. The vicar and his wife, gnarled and tanned from much gardening and birding in many parishes, took her shock and the relapses into silences that Allen would have recognized as what they were and saw instead grief and nostalgia. Ann was truly touched, but she wanted to shout "No! No! No!" She responded quite sincerely to their help and concern but felt so false while she did it.

One day, Amity looked her square in the face and said, "One thing seems very strange to me. Forgive me if I offend at such an unsettled time, but is your grief because you cannot grieve?"

"Oh, Amity, yes, yes, yes! He was so awful, and I left him because he frightened me so very much! Surely you've seen the villagers and their fear of him? They were so right to fear, Amity, so very right! Now I am terrified. Yes, that is what you are seeing so very clearly. I am terrified that if it is known that I hated him, was so very afraid of him, I will be accused of murdering him!"

"Oh, my dear! No one—*no one* would think you capable of such a thing. I have heard no such rumors anywhere, I promise you! Nor would I believe them if I did! Never!"

"Yes, and what about rumors that I have put, to quote Percival, 'my lover, Mr. Herrick,' up to it?"

"Ah yes, eventually we come to Percival and Mrs. Dray, do we not?"

"Yes, and her dear friend and dupe, Constable Stites."

"Well, we pray, and we do not behave in any way guiltily for we are not. I cannot believe that your relationship with our truly dear Mr. Herrick could possibly be in any way other than honorable. Further, you have just mentioned the only, and I repeat, the only ones in High Yews or anywhere else in this world who could possibly believe such a ridiculous story! This is only your poor nerves talking, my love."

"Oh, Amity!"

Ann simply broke down and cried and cried until all the fear poison was all drained out of her.

Amity Matthews never went anywhere without a sufficiency of handkerchiefs for all occasions. Since this was one of such great joy and relief, together, they used them all.

Chapter 27

Clearing The Debris

S oon, after the proverbial nine days, the wonder came to be not
that one person had shot Sir Arthur but that there had not
been a lynching party. The anonymous private secretary had
been found hiding and hiding with him many papers that he may
have hoped to find a profitable market for but reasonably should
have burnt. These papers supplied the keepers of the law with a long
list of suspects, both in the country and internationally. Rivalries
sprang up between units of the government, the Foreign Office,
Scotland Yard, and others, both in and out of England. The question
was now who would have the challenge and get the rewards in the
search for culprits. A further challenge involved keeping as much of
all this out of the public eye as possible. "Rumors abound" became
a commonplace phrase in the daily press. Unbelievable pressure was
put on anyone with a scrap of authority to do something, unspecified,
immediately. Scotland Yard was called in to deal with the murder, of
course, but there was so much more here than murder.

Scotland Yard, however, produced Superintendent Robert Oakes, a
trusted friend of Allen's since before the war. Dark haired, imposing,

with piercing gray eyes, he looked exactly like a Scotland Yard man on stage, a man anyone would recognize as intelligent, thoughtful, and good at chess. The skein was fast resembling a three-dimensional or, given the time element, a four-dimensional game of chess. Superintendent Robert Oakes was an excellent man to have on the case with Allen and the mysterious but charming Major Atherton.

The evidence found giving details of Sir Arthur's private life gave many a more sympathetic view of Ann in her new single life. Shocking, of course, but one could just see that a single woman with no family whatever could easily and without shame look to another man to share her joys and sorrows. Ann and Allen felt a little as though they had fallen into the century of Austen.

Mrs. Dray felt this to be only a minor setback and continued to spread more and more outlandish stories until they collapsed with the weight of their own fantasy. She looked askance not only at Ann and Allen, but also at Miss Makepeace and Charles Herrick combined. Sheer nonsense, of course, the common thought pronounced. The press became bored and left.

The FO was having more luck, together with more grief, as elements of certain foreign powers were found to be engaged in deals in armaments directly against the specific wording of treaties and signed letters of agreement.

Percival was not to be found. Reasons for Percival's retirement were found among Sir Arthur's papers, and a quiet search for the man himself was going forward with little luck. He was believed to be in France and, hopefully at least, well out of England.

Ann and Allen were granted a period of peace. Martha Appleby, the district nurse, was added to their circle of friends. She was a large woman, well muscled, with practice at turning of patients in beds and helping equally well-muscled elderly farmers up and down the narrow stairs of their cottages. She was a woman with much instinctive wisdom and a well-honed sense of good and evil. Nurse Appleby, sister to the village schoolmistress who shared her sense of good and evil, to the terror of the young, talked quietly with Allen for a while on one of her visits and then left the two to their own devices.

Ann could welcome Allen to her home with complete joy. She shook hands with him graciously in Nurse Appleby's presence, and Nurse Appleby was not in the least deceived.

Finally, Ann could ask, "What happened? I know he's dead, and that a shotgun was involved, and that it happened here by the stables on the night of the storm. Is Scotland Yard saying no more than that?"

Allen started talking in low tones when they heard Nurse Appleby talking loudly to someone evidently very close to the parlor windows. "I'm sure you have no call to be in those bushes, Mrs. Dray! Come out this instant and go on your way. No, you did not leave the button off your coat there, and if you had, I'd feel free to ask you just what the circumstances were at the time."

Unintelligible mumbling sounding remarkably like curses filtered through the shadows thrown by the bushes as they thrashed violently. "Come along now, that is enough of that!" It was clear that Nurse Appleby was going to stand her ground until Mrs. Dray was well out of sight and hearing. "All's clear," Nurse Appleby said loudly but to no one in particular.

Allen smiled but did not drop the subject Ann had raised.

"First of all, it has been confirmed that Sir Arthur Riddecoombe was the deceased, as you already know. Percival has been missing since Wednesday. Local thought is that Percy's non-presence rather clears that whole thing away. It does not. Not by a long shot. Ann, for God's sake, keep your guard up and your mouth closed! Since this is, from our point of view, a murder case pure and simple, well, maybe not that, but Scotland Yard is in charge. I've contacted Oakes there—he's as good as they come—and told him all I know. He'll be down tomorrow to take over officially. The unit I work with is theoretically military still and is concerned strictly on the international level. They, since that is their territory, are convinced that the murderer is from foreign lands and with foreign knowledge and approval. Maybe, maybe not. As far as I know, I'm the only one who sees both the local and the international perspective—the telescope and the microscope.

"I really do not think you are in any danger. That may be wishful thinking, but I do not think of myself as a wishful thinker. If I do wishful think, however, it is about you."

There was a brief pause in the conversation. Nurse Appleby was heard to be singing in the kitchen, and Vanguard was furious at a squirrel in the orchard. The feelings appeared to be mutual and the incident a standoff.

"We still have great reason to be discreet. This could blow up in our faces and become very nasty very fast." This he said after he had caught his breath. "Be your own strong, bright, brave self. The best thing you can do by far is write! Write as well as you can, and with every detail you can remember! I mean this! Use that writer's eye and get it all down on paper, whether it makes sense or not. If it does not make sense, don't try to force it. Use Letty as a sounding board, but trust your own instincts—always! The Powers that Be have a much longer line of sight than you do. They have some evidence on Sir Arthur, but they know nothing whatsoever about High Yews or you or anything on the personal level or the local level. This can be dangerous since these people are used to knowing everything and always are of the opinion that they know more than anyone else on anything. If they can't find the answer to a crossword puzzle, they consider that it is the puzzle's fault. These PtB are sure that you did not do it. Be glad for they have much influence. Be concerned because they are occasionally wrong. And when they are wrong, they are very, very wrong."

Allen stood with conviction and complete focus, as if he could hypnotize her into taking him with complete seriousness and absolute faith.

He only limped a little as he walked to the door.

Chapter 28

The Skein Returns

Ann wrote. She couldn't sit up yet for long periods of time to type, but she wrote on the good old yellow pads and in the exercise books. She started with the permanent inhabitants: the residents of High Yews and High Place Old Lodge. Oddly, the owners of the mansion on the hill, High Place, after such a battle to buy the gracious old place, seem to have disappeared. There was a story there too, Ann would wager, but not for now—not with so much else that was so very vitally important.

So. Percival. She could certainly write about Percival. She had to edit Percival severely. So much of what she first put down was spite. Or was it? Some of it she put back in. Stet, stet, ignore the crossings out. Leave as it was. Stet.

Letty was a godsend. Back from Scotland and swearing never to go see those aunts again ever in this world, she could read through the stets and write a clear copy that Ann would not be ashamed to show to the major. She wrote everything about Percival, and about Arthur too, that was by any possible fluke unknown to everyone in

High Yews. Not just that Arthur was a heel and a blackmailer. Not just that he had been a spiteful child with few friends but, as clearly as she could, whom he had tricked, whose belongings suddenly became the property of some other child or young man, most often Arthur himself.

Then she went on to the staff of High Place. At one time, Mrs. Dray had been quite close to Arthur. She had been the only one who could deal with his tantrums. Gradually, however, the High Place staff had come to realize that she was so good with Arthur because they were two of a kind. Mrs. Dray was laid off. Arthur had the tantrum of his life—up to that time. A series of new tutors had been hired, one after another, until finally Arthur had been sent to boarding school.

Ann tried to write two separate lists, one of suspects and one of victims. The lines became too tangled in the skein, and she had had to admit that a victim may have had to become a suspect eventually. On the other hand, a suspect might have been made to face his or her actions and had become Arthur's victim in the end. So Ann listed everyone as evenhandedly as she could. It was a struggle. One of the hardest parts was when Ann had gotten to the lists of pale shadowy visitors, and Letty had recognized her father.

"That does not mean he truly did anything wrong, Letty! Please! He may have been accused. Arthur may have tried to involve him, but that does not mean that he actually did anything criminal!"

Letty was inconsolable. Allen finally sat her down and talked like the proverbial Dutch uncle. "We have to work with fact and only fact. Yes, he was there. We have absolutely no way of knowing what happened after he went through those doors. Your father may have stood up to him. May have threatened him back. Arthur may have finally dropped him as a bad risk for any of a hundred reasons! We have to go on what we know—and only that! Now before this blew up, you were very, very valuable to us. Ann depends on you. Are you going to go into a ladylike decline and become a burden, or are you going to say, 'Well maybe he did do something wrong,' without a doubt not as wrong as Arthur made it seem, but wrong. The best—the only—thing you can do now is to help Ann and me and Major Atherton and Superintendent Oakes. For God's sake, make amends. Take this thing out into the clear light of day and right the wrongs! Are you up to this, or do we find someone at Scotland Yard and train her up to do what you already know? Letty, you know so many things that we don't know! Things we need to know! This whole project could fall through because you don't help us. Innocent people could be charged, and people like Percival go free—because of what you do or do not do. It's up to you Letty. It's a hard choice, believe me, I know. Which will it be? All the way, Letty. No halfway commitments. There is no such thing."

Letty stared at Allen. "I'm just helping with the typing and things. Nothing, really!"

"Oh no, you are not. You are a very vital part of this whole picture!"

"The skein," Ann said. "The skein, Letty. You and I have to do this together! It is hideously difficult, but it must be done! Oh please, Letty, please help us!"

Letty stared at the wall for a long time. "It may prove that what they thought about my father was true. I loved my father dearly. It would be like betrayal."

Allen had had enough. "All right, so you'd rather hide your father's faults and betray your country, is that it? Let us know honestly and right now, or else you are a danger to Ann, and I will not have that."

"Yes, yes, of course. Just give me a little time to grieve."

"You may not have anything to grieve over, Letty! Your father may have been one of Arthur's stumbling blocks. After all, he gave his life to show people that something was very wrong, didn't he? Can you see it that way? He may have been a coward all his life and finally found something that he could do to point the way for the rest of us."

"Thank you, Ann. All right, I'll keep going—but, oh, Ann!" Letty wept on Ann's shoulder, and Ann said all the things that she remembered Amity saying to her and wishing she had Amity's source of handkerchiefs.

"Good girl!" said Allen gruffly and handed Ann his larger and spotless man's handkerchief and let them work it out together.

The next person on Ann's list was Mrs. Dray. Together, Ann and Letty studied Mrs. Dray's activities and all her relationships with the others in the skein. How had she achieved her power? Who had been afraid of her? Did anyone have any idea why? So many times Mrs. Dray was just a big fat bluff that Letty began to think that bluff was a large part of the dynamics that had tied the skein into such terribly tight knots. So much of this was true that Ann let her keep her optimism, and they could work together more closely than before.

Ann told Letty of her terror of Percy's threats of a divorce case, something she wouldn't have done before. The truth, growing on them both, that so many people were caught in this concatenation gave them a feeling of a shared cause and added energy to their work.

Ann realized, as they continued to work on Arthur's guest lists at his little "weekends" and intimate gatherings, that she had not been nearly as stupid with names as Arthur had implied. He simply had not told her the names, or had spoken them while turned away from her, or left out an important one when it could have rung bells for Ann. Finally she realized that the whole scenario was just another way Arthur used to confuse her and keep her in her place. None of the names had to have been real names at all.

Oh, how much she had missed or had seen and not trusted because of her lack of faith in herself. She confided this to Letty, and somehow it made them both feel better. They learned to trust themselves and each other. The work went faster and faster. Ann learned to separate Ann-thought from Arthur-thought. If what Ann thought was really right, then Arthur-thought was at the very least highly suspect. The relief was intoxicating.

They began to connect cause and effect, to untangle one strand of yarn from another, to see how fear caused by Arthur tightened knots of fear or created knots where none really existed. So many strands. The sentences were going off the lines and up the sides of pages. Letty had to calm Ann down sometimes just to understand what she had written. Letty calming Ann down. A few months ago, it would have been unthinkable. They found new relationships.

Ann wanted to be able to run. Not to run away, but just to run as she had on the farm. To get the tension out and let her think more clearly—or just not think at all for a while.

Letty was not a runner. Sometimes Gil ran with her, and sometimes, when he could, Allen would, but his leg slowed him down even while it strengthened the muscles. At first, the idea of Ann's being out on the fields or in the little orchard was argued strongly against by the major and by Oakes of Scotland Yard when he heard of it, but gradually they came to see the tension that built up in Ann as she worked, and finally the gentlemen conferred and decided that it was better than insomnia or alcohol. They had gotten used to having women involved in war work, but Ann somehow was their Ann, and it was hard for them to fit her into their previous views of how things were to be done.

So Ann ran. Sometimes Ann and Allen ran together. Always there were men watching, Yard men mostly, who complained at first, but soon got used to the easy task. Sometimes the task became so easy they had to be warned that they were out there for Ann's health and not their own.

Nurse Appleby was a steadying influence. She knew so much about the villagers and the farmers in the community. She'd seen them born and many of them die.

Ann wondered at this little community, so isolated from the world, but so important in itself.

Chapter 29

Crops Threatened

The rural community of High Yews would protect itself at all costs—including people not directly involved in its life, like Miss Makepeace and Charles Herrick. Ann's writer's imagination saw the village as a community barn. If there was a rat found in the barn, even the most moral of them, especially the most moral of them, might see it as a duty to protect the whole against the invader, the spoiler of the community integrity.

Nurse Appleby would protect those she had midwifed into this—not into this world so much as into this community. This community was their world. All the knowledge of each member of the community was filed both in the old battered metal filing cabinets at the cottage hospital and in the live cabinets of their minds. Would the most moral of them be the ones to watch, not the least moral? The right, to them, would be the best thing for the whole. Not a world war as she saw it—as Allen and the major and now the superintendent saw it. They would see this community as their own world! Would they take this—had they taken this into their own hands, their own world? With Arthur as the rat in their own barn? No! Put that thought far away! Far, far away.

Yet the killing of Sir Arthur had had a remarkably stable influence on the little community. Like the opening of a window to the sunshine and a fresh, clean wind flowing over the fields of clover and young corn. Nurse Appleby's comments on Sir Arthur had left no doubt of her opinions. Nor was there any doubt of the courage of her convictions and her commitment to the health of the community. There was no doubt at all that Sir Arthur had seriously threatened the health of the community of High Yews. No doubt whatsoever.

Mrs. Matthews, just passing by, looked in on a distraught Ann crying and rubbing her forehead feverishly.

Mrs. Matthews was by nature and profession a comforter. Quickly she came to Ann and took her hands, cooing and making those soft sounds that do so well to comfort a baby with no understanding of the sometimes fearsome new world around him.

"Now, now. There, there, it can't be a bad as all that, now, not really!" Realization came to Amity that it could be as bad as all that—had been as bad as all that. The first thing to do was to calm Ann and comfort her into quietness. "Can you just tell me a little bit so I can understand and help?"

"Oh, Mrs. Matthews!"

"Amity, please, my love! So much easier to say, don't you think? Now do excuse me, so many distractions. Do go on!"

Ann drew a deep breath. Surely not Amity!

Oh, Mrs . . . Amity, I'm just so afraid. You see, I know so little about the people here. I only know I didn't kill Arthur!"

It was as good a place to start as any and told Amity much about Ann. "No, but you don't know who did, and it could really be any of us. Or is it that you do know? That your lists have shown you something?"

"No, no. I don't know at all. I just had the thought that it could be someone not just who hated Arthur but someone who loves High Yews and is so dedicated to protecting it that the only way they could see to do it would be to kill. It would be—to that person—as simple as saving the corn by killing the rat in the barn. Could it be like that?"

"Well! That is certainly a wise thought. I'm happy to say I don't think it's quite accurate, thank heavens. You've come to suspect everyone, haven't you? That is a very frightening thought!" Amity was silent for a moment. "Very frightening indeed! It would be like an amputation, wouldn't it? To save the whole person? Yes, indeed. If I didn't know these people as well as I do, and, of course, as you don't, I would be running to Timothy this minute. And you don't have a Timothy, do you, you poor dear! Except that nice Mr. Herrick, of course. Oh yes, well, if that is a secret, it stays a secret with us at the vicarage until you feel comfortable with telling the rest of us for that is none of our telling. I really do think you can trust him, don't you? Why don't you talk it over with him? He seems so knowledgeable. Quiet, perhaps too quiet, but I'm sure that is war nerves, and I'm sure he would improve with knowing, my dear."

Amity stopped to draw breath and pat Ann gently on the back since she seemed to be choked with tears. So understandable. Imagine suspecting an entire community! "I'll just get us some cold fresh water and put the kettle on, if I may, dear?"

Ann nodded, speechless.

When Amity returned, having given Ann a little time to compose herself, she saw that Ann was much improved. She even had a smile on her face!

A little later, Nurse Appleby, after a quiet conversation with the vicar's wife, came by with some hot chicken soup and a list of things for Ann to go over so she could give it to the grocer's boy.

"My aunt Emily had a rat once," she remarked casually, causing Ann to spill some of the good soup. "For her hair, your know. That's what they call those little bits of hair in a net that they would wind their own hair around to make it look like they had a, what do they call it, a French something. At any rate, it was false, and it looked false. Nonsense, I call it. I must say I like your hair now that you've let it go back to normal. It has such a lovely natural curl to it, now it's shorter. I'm glad to see you eat up that soup. Eating's important, especially after the kind of shock you've had." Nurse sat calmly crocheting while she watched her patient eat. "The custard's all anyhow after the ride over, but the taste's the same. I never thought I'd see a fresh nutmeg again in my life, but I found some over in Bridgeport. Real nutmeg, not that carved kind either. I don't know who they think they're fooling."

Ann smiled as she savored the custard and thought of the long winter nights when Yankee peddlers carved "nutmegs" and dyed them with walnut juice to sell to unsuspecting New England housewives in the spring. She had always wondered about that. A nutmeg smells so very much different from a black walnut! More falseness. It took a canny housewife!

Ann hoped she would turn into a canny writer and not let her imagination get away with her when she needed a clear head as she did now.

Nurse Appleby noticed the smile. "Smiles mean an early mending, I've always said." She got up to collect the dishes. "No," she said as Ann pushed back her chair to help. "Take your rest where you find it. I'm here just to take a little of the load of your shoulders for a bit. Might as well enjoy it. You do work hard at that writing of yours!"

Later, in the twilight by the fire in the kitchen, Ann drowsed over her latest entries into the strange and growing skein. Movement by the kitchen door. Allen was furious! "That should have been locked and bolted!"

"Even against you?"

"I'm not the only one out there, Ann!"

He paused only long enough to make sure of every lock and every bolt, then he turned to her. "Ann!"

Ann too knew how to give comfort. Together they held each other, rocking from side to side like exhausted dancers in an hours-long marathon. No words, just that tender, gentle rocking, as if they were each other's babies comforting the other baby from a midnight nightmare. Just the steady calming, strengthening, being there for each other in the flickering firelight.

After a while, Ann asked, "Would you like to see my homework? It's coming along so fast I scared myself today."

Allen had trouble coming to the surface. "He knows more than he did yesterday, and he's worried too."

Allen sat down in his chair and she in her chair. She watched him as he read the new pages, the new arrangement of people on each page. She leaned back, encouraging him to relax. He did not relax. Wordlessly, he reached for the last set of sheets. The total skein covered ten pages by now. Ann thought it deserved to be capitalized now that it had become so important. That was probably foolish, only a writer's pride. Still, she smiled at the conceit as she watched Allen.

When he did lean back finally, it was not to relax.

What does he see that I didn't? Ann wondered.

He put his feet up on the coffee table and spread the sheets out on his legs. "Ann, do you know what a war room is?"

"I think so. I mean, it's where they play war games, isn't it?" Ann knew full well how childish that sounded.

"In sandboxes with plastic platoons, yes." Allen smiled at last. "The point is that they use very important and secret information as well presented as this is, if they are lucky. Great care is taken so that they can do all this in very secret places where the information they are working with, and they themselves, are very, very safe. Where you should be right now."

He got up and went out to the phone, muttering to himself. "Which first? Damn it, which first?" Quickly, he dialed Oakes's Scotland Yard private line. "Thank God. Listen, how soon can you get Ann into a safe house? Yes, I mean now, tonight! Not good enough. Work on it, could you? Damnation, of course it's important! I'm calling UQ headquarters now. Yes, I know you don't coordinate. You don't even cooperate, but this covers both pidgins. It has to. Do you want to be in charge, or do you want him to do it? All right then. Now. Yes, now. I don't care who you have to call. It's that or lose both of us. I'm serious. Those papers are vital, and Ann's more vital than that."

There was a tapping at the window. "We have a situation here, yes, Ann's house, right now! ASAP!"

The line went dead.

The tapping continued.

"All right in there? Only, you know, it's only old vicar and Amity, you know, our bird-watching outfit, and there's something going on out here. We wanted you to know, don't you know."

Ann shook with laughter and fear meeting head-on with exhaustion. "Allen?"

This time she knew Allen was there because his hand was over her mouth.

No. She must not respond.

Another voice. Amity?

"Ann dear, I most humbly do apologize. Well, I do. Too much time on my hands and too much Miss Marple. I just . . ." Now there was the definite impression of a hand over Amity's mouth as well. Ann prayed to God that it was the vicar's. Did she now need saving, or was the outside like the inside—two strong women with their still stronger men keeping them from speech. Whichever it was, why was it? What in heaven's name had gotten them into such a bizarre situation?

Then glass shattered. Allen shoved Ann down behind the sofa. Old vicar's voice was going farther and farther away. Something about heading them off somewhere?

This was ridiculous. "Damn, damn, double damn, going to smear my head with jam!" The old childish atrophic warding-off chant seemed to have worked. Hadn't it? Bright lights of all colors, beautiful blues and reds flooding the leaves of the tree outside. Except her arm hurt. She was lying on it, and it hurt!

"Allen, what?"

Allen had run out into the flowing light. "The Matthews, they went that way! See if they're safe! Get the medicos, Ann's down. Yes, in here."

"Ann, Ann, come back now." It was Allen's voice. She had never heard it so gentle, so warm! It had all the comfort in the world! She turned her head quickly to find him. Too quickly. Her head swam. She reached out for his hand. Wrong hand. The other, when she tried again, worked much better. She fell into his eyes and floated there, afraid to blink for fear he'd disappear. This time, he stayed.

"Slowly, gently, my love. You seem to have survived in excellent form this time."

"This time! Allen!" She could tell from last time that she was numb with relief, the blessed relief from the pain she now knew would come later.

Allen was here! Her relief was overwhelming. Slowly her eyes closed and her head fell over Allen's protecting arm.

Chapter 30

Deceptive Changes In The Wind Patterns

A nurse had come running at the sound of Ann's raised voice.

"Good morning! I'm glad to hear the patient is awake and in good form!"

Damn all cheerfulness, thought Ann.

"Just let me take your vitals, my dear, while I'm here, and then we'll not bother you for a while." Deftly, the nurse moved between Ann and Allen.

"Not my vitals, you're not! I'm still using them." Ann panicked. All the little gold pins that she had seen on a nurse's uniform since she had been fascinated by them as a child were missing!

"Allen! She's not a nurse! Stop her!"

Very quickly and very quietly, Allen took the nurse by the arm and led her out of Ann's room. "Police! Here! Now! Where is the man who is supposed to be on this door? I want him here now!" It took longer than "now" for the noise to settle down.

Finally, Allen showed enough people in charge his identifications, several of them. Unfortunately the "nurse" had no identification whatsoever and was taken to police headquarters to explore this omission.

"Stites! They had Stites protecting her?"

Ann could barely recognize his voice. Ice formed.

"As of this minute, Stites is wanted for questioning in this case, do you understand me? No, I do not believe he 'went for a coffee just down the hall.' In hell he did. Where is Scotland Yard? Where is a phone? Never mind, I know his number!"

Ann wondered, still a little groggy, if she had a warranty on her life. Could she borrow one of Van Eyck's?

"At Woodside Hospital. Code UQ 6, Colonel Allen Herrick requesting. Thank you. I will be in room 203. Yes, I still want Constable Stites, if he should still be in the building, which I sincerely doubt. What idiot put him on this case in the first place? On whose orders? Yes, I request a copy of those orders. Also that the originals be fingerprinted. That's Colonel Herrick. Superintendent Oakes will confirm. Yes, ASAP!"

"Yes." He said this to another voice. "There was a young woman here a minute ago posing as a nurse and gaining access to a restricted area. She has unfortunately escaped."

The door opened again, and Allen came in with an older man, tall, stooped, with the look of a retired military man.

"Dr. Hallton here, miss. Sorry for the bit of a hassle."

Allen's voice cut through sharply. "Thank you for attending to this yourself, but the situation was beyond a 'hassle,' as you chose to call it. It was dangerous and must be considered potentially an attack on the life of Lady Riddecoombe."

"It's like that, is it? Oh, dear! I'd not realized, of course."

"Top priority, sir. I have requested Superintendent Oakes, Scotland Yard CID, to send a dependable replacement for Stites, who should never have been allowed in this hospital, and have requested a search for the young woman posing as a nurse. She should be considered armed and dangerous. It is extremely doubtful that she is working alone."

"Good Lord! Bad as that! That's bad, very bad! Next thing you know, we'll be needing our own police force just for the hospital, don't you know. Well, I expect that'll be for you."

Allen politely asked Hallton to stay with Ann as he answered the phone at the desk.

"'Fraid our place has rather let you down, young lady."

"Not at all, Dr. Hallton. I've been made quite comfortable."

Ann began to be fond of this retired military man. His white mustache was very white and very impressive, but it would never wave with any grace or be blown out with a voice of any commanding authority.

Allen returned with a full budget of news. Oakes would be there shortly. Evidently, Constable Stites would be returning as well—by ambulance. He had speeded over a curve that should never have been speeded over and might not recover consciousness.

Oakes arrived and promptly took charge. The war had aged men rapidly. Oakes was much more thoughtful than he looked at first glance and much deeper. He had a habit of staring off into space when he thought that made him look absentminded. This was not the case. His mind was right there. His mind was deeper than you realized until he spoke—or played chess with you.

Will Evans, his sergeant, was just at acceptable height for the force, full of energy and humor. He was always there when needed, but never in the way. His smile was, at least partly, because Oakes had all the responsibility.

Oakes gave orders for the car that had crashed to be inspected thoroughly and checked for prints. "Not much hope, but you never know." Stites was to be put in a private room, and a guard was to be kept to take down whatever mutterings Stites might give them, however unintelligible they were to the sergeant.

Ann, tiring rapidly, was obsessed with the thought that Allen and Oakes, two strong, independent man who were accustomed to acting quickly and on their own, might find it extremely difficult to work together. Allen, sensing her distress but not knowing the cause, went to the bed and gently lifted her hand.

"So, milady, what disturbs your however infinitesimal peace?"

"I love you."

"And does this disturb your rest?"

"No! Well, yes! Stay safe, my love! Please work well with Oakes! Hear me when you work with him. Will you? Your fingers feel cold. You are so very tired. I am so very tired too," she said groggily.

Allen envied her for a brief minute and then followed Oakes out the door.

Oakes drew the door behind them quietly. "This is DS Anderson. He'll keep a good watch on your lady while we find somewhere private to talk. Very private."

They walked down the hall, not a word between them.

Chapter 31

Oakes And Lightning

O akes leaned back in the large chair, the chair of a doctor's authority behind a doctor's desk. He nodded to Allen. "Good to see you."

"And you, sir." Allen smiled. "What exactly happened?"

"Damned if we know, Herrick! Damned if we know! We got wind of some foreign johnnies, real spy stuff, coming into the picture after Riddecoombe's papers were found, which, I must say, we all thought had been kept very much under cover. There's a mole somewhere, damn it all!"

"I know," said Allen quietly. "I've been after him for some time now. That's what led me to Riddecoombe. What in the name of all that's holy is the logic of the link from Riddecoombe to Ann? She is in it at the local level without a doubt, but not at the international level. I'm positive of that. Percival is a go-between, between the French connection and the English. It really is as though there are two of him. He travels back and forth carrying messages."

"These johnnies at the international level, ours and theirs, just because they're flying so high, sometimes lose sight of the ground. Sometimes lose their oxygen too, if you know what I mean. These boys, whoever they are, crashed from a great height, so to speak. What they thought they were doing firing at Ann is anyone's guess.

"They just missed the vicar too. As well not tell Ann that one. On the basis of information received, we understood that they were headed for High Place Old Lodge. That's where we were waiting for them at any rate."

"Received from whom? Oakes, this is hugely important! You were told a lie. Wrong in the first place, but the important thing here is that you were lied to. Who did it?"

"I'll follow that back. You are right. It makes no sense." Oakes paused on the doorway. "Hope your lady's not too bad."

Allen smiled. "She's braver and stronger and smarter than she'll let you see. Incidentally. Oh god! The skein! The papers at her house! What happened to them? That's the crux of the whole thing, I'm sure of it."

"Papers? We looked over the house pretty thoroughly, I thought, but we found nothing that looked relevant to the case."

"Have you even spoken with Major Atherton?"

"Oh, yes, you mean that list Ann wrote up? Yes, most useful!"

"It's gone a lot farther than that list by now. If UQ has it and is not showing it to Scotland Yard or the Foreign Office, U Q has the mole! Unit Q is where the danger is coming from at the international level. That means we have a huge problem, and lives—I hate to think how many lives—are at stake. For God's sake, have someone you trust go over the house again!"

A fresh young face showed in a bare crack in the door. So much for privacy. "Those orders, sir, the ones for Stites to be on duty? The signature is just a scrawl. That's all you can expect from these doctors, sir."

"That was not a medical order! That was a police order! The name and the officer number code should have been clear as day! I'll have someone's hide for that one!"

Oakes was furious.

Allen was ice cold. "Give me that order."

"Sorry, sir, it's still at the desk. I didn't think you'd need—seriously, it's just a scrawl!"

"Didn't think! Get it now!"

Allen and Oakes ran back to Ann's room. From far down the hall, they could hear the uproar. Allen ran ahead of Oakes with the older man at his heels. Major General Sir Grayson Hoving was fierce, frantic, and emphatic! He was to be allowed into Ann's room immediately!

Detective Sergeant Anderson, a large young man on the station's hammer throw team, was caught between his orders and this man's obvious seniority and intensity. He decided to obey orders, earning himself a promotion.

Allen, coming up abruptly, was equally fierce and intense. "Hoving!"

Senior Security officers were never in the field. That was one of the first rules for the security of the entire unit! Yet here in a public hospital corridor was Major General Sir Grayson Hoving of Unit Q himself raving like a madman!

Allen had to think. He had to stop everything else in his brain and think. It was impossible. It was in front of his face. Hoving, on whom everything in UQ depended, had gone around the bend. There was, as of this moment, effectively no UQ. None. In Hoving's mind, there was only Hoving, nothing else. Hoving must be the mole!

"What the hell, Hoving!"

The ranting man turned on Allen.

"You would do well to remember that I outrank you by several degrees and many years, Herrick." The man was purple in the face and panting with rage. "If you hadn't betrayed me with that young hussy, none of this would have been necessary—and you know it! Oh, yes, Percival has told me all about you and your lovebird—the little lovebird who has turned you to the other side! She must be dealt with! No more secrets of international importance can be allowed to slip through your fingers into her hands! You used to be faithful to UQ, Herrick! You were a good man! We did so much together to help save our country! Oh, the damage a woman can do!"

Allen was stunned. Here was his mole! His own chief officer—the head of Unit Q, accusing Ann of leaking secrets? The man was truly mad. Allen was thinking back over the work the two of them had done together, good work. Good work for their country! Hoving was absolutely right so far. But Hoving had counted Allen's relationship with himself as more important than his loyalty to his country! Impossible! Hoving could only see that Allen had transferred his—his what?—his allegiance, his affection, to Ann. In Hoving's mind, all allegiance was owed to himself—all loyalty belonged to Hoving and to Hoving alone! In Hoving's twisted reasoning, Allen's love for Ann amounted to treason! Hoving was the source of danger to Ann! To his country! Unthinkable! Yet here it was in front of him!

Allen turned aside, unable to look at this trembling, raving, man. A man past all rational thought. This man he had once trusted implicitly. Trusted with his life.

Oakes intervened. "That does not give you immunity to Scotland Yard within the boundaries of this country, sir. I am putting you under arrest until your handwriting can be confirmed."

Oakes had seen Allen's thought here and was going on a seasoned officer's instinct. "Am I to assume that you are resisting arrest?"

"Arrest? By that young pipsqueak? I'll have you know that the young woman in that room has information that is absolutely vital to the security of this country! Vital, man, vital! By the authority of Unit Q, I demand entry!"

"That would be resisting arrest, causing a public nuisance, and impeding an officer in the performance of his duty." Calmly and with precision, Oakes was making out his paperwork. "I'll have to ask you to come with me, sir, if you will."

"Never! That young woman has vital information. If it were to get out, it would be a national disaster! You cannot have the slightest understanding!"

"Yes, sir, so I understand. Now you don't want all these good people to be privy to all this vital information, do you, sir?"

Hospital attendants were quietly gathering around the irate little man, first to see the excitement and then more seriously to take a professional interest in what might be their next assignment. Another doctor on the floor was quietly on the phone at the desk. "Code blue, code blue, floor 2, west wing" rang out over the intercom.

A new doctor came through the doors at a fast clip. He stopped at the edge of the group and talked quietly but hurriedly with Herrick, watching Hoving as he listened.

Finally, he stepped to the vortex of the furor and calmly introduced himself. "I am Dr. Rotherington of psychiatric medicine, sir, and I am admitting you to the psychiatric ward of this hospital for observation. Yes, I have that authority, sir. Yes, I am noting that this action is being taken without the patient's consent. Nevertheless, I see it as my responsibility, seeing the situation as I am seeing it at present, that I proceed along the lines I have just described to you." Motioning to the three attendants, the doctor led the now-screaming

Hoving to the area marked No Admittance. The door had been locked and padded. It was now waiting only for the doctor to be securely locked again.

"My heartfelt thanks, Doctor," Allen spoke quietly and gratefully as the psychiatrist went by. "Do not neglect to empty his pockets. There is always a chance, you know."

"I shall also relieve him of his tie, belt, and shoelaces. Yes, sir. I too am a professional."

"Of course, please excuse my emotional response." Allen ran a shaking hand through his hair. "The young lady in question, well, it's rather important to me personally, sir."

Rotherington smiled as he quickly went by. "I am a psychiatrist. I understand that too."

Chapter 32

Shelter From The Storm

Allen stumbled in his hurry to open the door to Ann's room. He limped badly as he came up to Ann, sitting up in her bed now, listening to the noise level return to normal. Normal, that is, for a hospital.

"Allen, are you all right? Safe, I mean? It hasn't been very restful, has it?" She held her hand out to him. Then she saw his face.

He slumped in the chair by her bed and rested his head on her hand. "Safe house, safe house," He murmured over and over, rubbing his forehead across her fingers. "Must get you to a safe house! Oh, Ann, it was so close! I hadn't realized! I hadn't seen it, Ann!"

She stroked his hair and made Amity noises, except they were Allen and Ann noises—special to them alone. "I do love you so much! So much more than I can say!"

A detective sergeant knocked on the door. Ann growled. She needed to protect her man and to have him protect her.

"Sir, the patient was found to have a syringe possibly of potassium of cyanide on his person. Superintendent Oakes asked me to tell you. The patient is being transferred to St Joseph's."

"Tell the superintendent thanks! I owe him."

"Right, sir." The young man smiled. "That'll be a relief, right enough."

Oakes came soon to report on the upheaval at UQ and the changes that seemed, now, to be happening all so very quickly. The unit seemed to have imploded with the charges against Major General Hoving. Allen repeated to Oakes his decision to leave UQ no matter who else remained in the unit or what remained of the unit itself. They talked into the small hours, comparing one man to another, one talent to another, one man's governing abilities to another's.

Finally, Oakes left after all the talk, thankful that the final decisions were not theirs to make, and enormously thankful that Allen had made the decision to join forces with the Yard.

"Allen, if I'm in a safe house, where will you be?"

Allen brought himself back with a jerk.

"Oh, I'll be here and there, you know, doing my job."

"Which job, Allen?"

Trust Ann to go straight to the heart of the thing.

"The war is over. Working with the people who think it is still on is working with people who are not living in reality. We found that out with Hoving. I learned that lesson the hard way—a nightmare of a hard way. I am through with that life. I think I told Letty once—there is no such thing as a divided commitment." Allen's rueful smile held such pain it tore at Ann's heart. "I should have listened. I've worked with, cooperated with, the Yard, for a number of years. They might find a place for me. We're a lot like shoemakers, you know. Once you learn a trade, you may change masters, but you stick to what you know. The shoemaker sticks to his last. It's a pun. The 'last' is the wooden shape the shoemaker uses to mold the leather onto the shape of a particular foot. It can also mean 'to his last breath.' There's no question I'm out of espionage. Scotland Yard has positions that can make good use of the skills I have without all the cloak-and-dagger mentality I've had to deal with. It was necessary during the war. The war is over. Long live the peace!"

Chapter 33

Ashes As Evidence

O akes knew where to find Herrick. He knew he had to report that the skein was missing, except that it probably was the small pile of ashes just found in Ann's kitchen fireplace. Briefly, with no apologies, the superintendent reported the failure of Scotland Yard to save the precious document. "All burnt to a crisp. Can you work with us to reconstruct what we can?"

Ann looked at him with stark horror reflected in her face. All that work! "Even the carbons? Even my bed?"

"What does your . . . bed?" Oakes ran back out the door, skidded around the nurse's desk, and picked up the phone. "Seems as though your bed may yet be safe."

Allen grinned at Ann. He was gray in the face, but he still grinned.

She grinned back, but shushed him so she could hear Oakes.

"Yes, yes, under the bed."

"Go tell him *in* the mattress." Ann pushed Allen toward the door.

"Right. Right. Yes!. Well, cut it open, you clod!"

"Found! All of it? Ann, all of it there?"

"Yes!"

"Then we have it! We have it all!"

Oakes came back through the door a changed man. "The AC says a safe house for you both. The same house, if you don't mind. Yes, I thought you'd be pleased. I stressed economy to the AC. Then we get down to going over it all with you and our best men, and we'll make something of this mess yet!"

"Superintendent, listen to me!" Ann's voice had a new authority of her own. "Someone who is still close to us, somewhere we don't know about, whose name we don't know, set that fire. If I hadn't hidden the copy inside the mattress, we would have lost it all. Lost it all because of someone who is hidden to us and could do heaven knows what at any time. The fact is that you don't, literally, don't have a clue. Letty worked hand in glove with me on this. She needs protection as well. As evidently do my holdings at home. I'd suggest letting Gil and Letty take over the house and grounds with plenty of security while we are at this safe house of yours. The focus of the chase is now for one murderer, not for the safety of the civilized world, is that not so? Granted, one murderer, but one who for some reason feels he has to kill me? Why?"

"One of the men you saw at the lodge was an international mole. One who knows me by sight. I just met up with him in the hall. He was raving that you were giving important information from me to 'the enemy.' The war is still on for him. He made assumptions about our relationship, aided and abetted I would guess by Percival. My bet is that Percival set the fire.

"The skein still has much work to do. You saw things you didn't know you saw when you watched those cars come and go."

Oakes, sobered, said slowly, hesitantly, "I didn't want to tell you this so soon, but one of the men was definitely Professor Hampton-Gray. For another thing, one of the men you saw most often, and recognized not at all, was Percival Riddecoombe. Yes, hard to believe, isn't it? I do not know how they managed it, but sometimes a man would go, and another man would go with him. Did you realize that? Did you see, ever, two men in the same car? Probably the saddest of the men you saw go. The ones who were not seen again. Or not recognizably so. The second man, the one who got into the backseat, was, we are reasonably sure we can make a good case, was Percival—the one we were so sure had no connection with Sir Arthur's activities. The one we were so sure was in France at exactly that time. Ann, I'm very sorry."

"Oh God! Oh!" Ann wept. "I saw that happen. Oh, Allen!" She reached blindly for his hand. "The man wasn't just tired, just resting his head in his hands. He was praying! Praying not to be killed. And they killed him!"

Oakes and Allen looked at each other over Ann's bowed head.

"God, I hate this job!"

"Herrick, hang on with it, man. At least until we have this last job cleaned up! I ask nothing more of you, either of you, after that. And you two are the only ones who can help us make this happen! You two are the only ones who can do this thing, do you realize how important that is? CID, Scotland Yard, all of Scotland Yard, will give you all the help and support we can, believe me! But you are essential! You have to be the ones to help us do this thing. After that, you have a job at the Yard waiting for you. As quiet and peaceful a job as you want. Janitor? The highest paid janitor in the world? The janitor with the highest security in the world? You have it!"

Ann was gripping Allen's hand very, very hard. She was also watching Oakes very closely. He smiled back, this time more gently and sympathetically.

"The first thing is to separate as much as we can the foreign and the strictly local.

We'll get on that part ASAP. The continental aspects go to InterPol and out of our hair. We three need to work on the local aspects. Specifically, Sir Arthur's murder, and the attempts on Ann's life. The minute Ann can be transferred to a safe house, you will both go there. Now I'd like to spend some time here going through the skein and making decisions on what needs to be done by the Yard and how fast it needs to be done. Are you with me?"

Wordlessly, they both nodded.

Chapter 34

An Intense High Stalling Over
The Midlands

S o it began, the unraveling of the skein.

Two copies of the entire skein were dittoed in an office at the Yard. A very high security office. By a very high security office staff. Finally, it was rushed to Ann's hospital room by a very high security courier. At each step, the possibilities for interception were enormous. Their only hope was that the one person who had burned the original manuscript still thought that there had been only one manuscript, a little pile of ash in an otherwise bare fireplace.

Oakes got as comfortable as he could in a hospital chair. He was afraid if they gave him one of those reclining things, he'd fall asleep and miss the one point on which the whole thing might be hanging. He and Allen both had copies of the manuscript in front of them. Ann had hers in her head. To Allen, that was terrifying.

"Now tell me, chicks! All of it. Where to begin, and who's to start? Ann, it's your brainchild."

Evans came in quietly and sat in a corner, taking down all Ann said. Slowly, she went over each person, each interaction, when it happened, what seemed to be the results of what happened, who acted, and who were affected. All the dynamics, all the dimensions she had seen. Two hours later, another sergeant spelled Evans, but the talking went on and on. Allen broke in when he had something to add. They developed a rhythm.

When they broke for meals, Oakes studied the sergeants' notes and scribbled his next questions and comments. They began again. Over and over they worked deeper into the complexities of the skein. At first it was hard to separate the purely local from the international. Then they caught the connections that were completely local, and the focus intensified. Each watched the others as they spoke and tried to fit what they heard into what they knew that the others might not have known. It was slow and exhausting work done by exhausted people. Each interrupted only when they thought the time was right to insert their contribution. They spoke quickly and concisely and then listened intently to the questions from the others. The time line became interwoven, and the stories became more and more complex. At times it seemed as though there were two of each person. Percival, especially, seemed to shift and double and split.

Finally, Oakes looked at a very quiet Ann and saw that she was asleep. He got up quietly and motioned Allen to follow him out of the room. Allen, who had realized for some time the reason for Ann's quietness, nodded and followed.

Oakes strode down the hall, a hunter on a trail. The nurses, accustomed to urgency, moved automatically out of his way. When they reached the parking lot, Oakes asked if Allen were willing to continue the late hours at the Yard. Allen well knew the need pressing on them both to continue. He nodded, and they returned to Oakes's office at the Yard, sergeant still in tow, and went at it until the two men could do no more without the focus the job needed. Allen slept on

Oakes's little couch set up for such overnight necessities, and Oakes sat and sat and stared at his notes until they swam in his eyes and he too slept.

Morning saw Oakes giving orders, setting up new lines of investigation and communication, and reading the everlasting reports. Allen woke to the smell of office coffee and joined Oakes at his desk for a recap of the night's work.

Overnight, Oakes had organized his plan of attack. Still more of the action was delegated to organizations in other countries. The military and the Foreign Office could fight as much as they liked. Not Scotland Yard's pidgin. Thank the Lord.

Chapter 35

High Intensifies Over The West Country

High Place Old Lodge was one crime scene. Ann's house at the old Thatcher place, or rather her stable yard, was the other. Oakes began at High Place Old Lodge with the housekeeper, Miss Agnes Tilly. There was there he put his foot wrong. Ann could have told him. First, he should have spoken to Braithwaite at the outset. Second, he should have known that a woman who had been a housekeeper for as long as Miss Tilly had been a housekeeper without receiving any form of the honorary *Mrs.* was not worth the powder.

Braithwaite, unfortunately, was out. Agnes Tilly, unfortunately, was in. She, as usual, was doing nothing. As usual, that nothing was so important that the superintendent was forced to cool his heels until his temper was too hot to keep them cool anymore. Once found, Agnes was inescapably the Agnes whom Ann had described so devastatingly in the skein. Tall, gray, and trembling, she resembled a Lombardy poplar in a high wind. Her glasses were of a high degree of magnification—so high that one could not see her, much less she see the person before her.

Ann's sketch immediately came to mind and stayed there. The hair carried out the poplar theme by being a gray that had been bleached so often that it had developed a kind of verdigris tint all its own. One could be pardoned for expecting it to rustle in that imaginary high wind. Lipstick so vibrant that it appeared to extend several inches in front of her pallid powdered face did not add to her authority. Nor did it add to her attempt at an aura of grief. The idea that she, Agnes Tilly, had anything to do with the planning of her master's death was ridiculous.

As she herself said in strident tones, "Ridiculous! An insult!" Did the deepness of her mourning give the police officer no indication of the shock she had suffered? Certainly his widow was not dressed as she was! "Widow indeed!"

No, Ann would not have been caught dead. Oakes winced as he thought it in a shapeless, washed-out, multiple-use rag of varying grays and unintended greens.

A set of jet beads, real but uncared for, completed the ensemble. No rings of any kind were seen on the useless claws. Will found himself doodling in the margins of his notebook. He was good. He could be cruel.

A shaken but very cooperative Braithwaite was, once found, as helpful as was possible. Ann's leaving High Place Old Lodge had been a blow to Braithwaite, leaving him with Miss Tilly to assume all the duties of the housekeeper. The longer the butler had to work with Agnes Tilly, the fonder grew his memories of "his Lady Anne."

He was more than eager to help especially when he heard that his Lady Anne was safe and out of harm's way.

While Miss Tilly pleaded an ignorance that rang all too true. Braithwaite could deal with fact and immediately became Oakes's friend.

Miss Tilly fell back as if she had been struck.

"Gun room! You are well aware that the room is always kept locked!"

"Yes, Miss Tilly. That is why we need the keys."

"I am sure you've seen the gun room before! I mean, surely! I remember it quite well! Oh, yes! All those young men rummaging around in there! The racket!"

Oakes looked at Braithwaite meaningfully. Braithwaite responded, "Miss Tilly, I have promised the superintendent all possible cooperation from the entire staff. Now what seems to be the trouble?" He had heard trouble from the pantry—heard it all too clearly from the pantry.

"Oh, oh, dear, I do feel so unwell! I do beg your pardon!"

Miss Tilly fled in the face of what Oakes was coming to suspect she considered the enemy. Interesting. A further word was in order. Oakes pondered briefly on which sergeant deserved such an assignment. As usual, he decided he would have to do it himself. Damn. Always the sticky ones. Sometimes they came unglued in informative ways.

Braithwaite, every inch of his body showing his distress and disapproval and his deepest apologies, begged to be told how he might be of assistance. Oakes, still watching the flight of Miss Tilly thoughtfully, replied that all he required was the set of keys to the gun room.

"Apart from the set you received when you were here last, superintendent, there is only my own set, which I have with me at all times. If you will just follow me." So the superintendent was graciously put in his place, and the superintendent learned that there were only the two sets of keys—two sets that anyone was willing to tell him about. He would have bet serious money that there was at least one more set.

Braithwaite unlocked the doors and stepped aside.

"If you'll just stay a bit, Braithwaite, you may be of still further help to me."

Braithwaite would enjoy being any help at all as long as it meant being where he could watch significant people doing significant things.

Superintendents were not allowed hunches. Nevertheless, somehow, Oakes felt that this room held an important clue, one that had been overlooked previously. Maybe he was catching it from Ann, this intuition that was so very hard to describe. Silently he stood in the center of the room and rotated full circle.

Braithwaite, seeing this as a new police method he had not known of before, held his breath. Next, the super went over the walls with their racks of highly polished cherished rifles, pistols, revolvers, and the spot without dust where the shotgun had been kept. There was one other dust-free spot among the pistols and revolvers.

"Is there something on these shelves that you would expect to find here that seems to be missing?" The superintendent waited. Braithwaite looked.

"Several things, sir. I see that they are missing but am at a loss as to how to explain the fact."

"Try."

"Well, of course, there is the spot where the lesser of Sir Arthur's shotguns should be. The dust surrounding the spot, most unfortunately, makes that embarrassingly clear. Perhaps more disturbing, sir, is the fact that the space where his government-issue revolver should stand is in a similar condition."

Oakes smiled the smile of a cat enjoying unexpected cream.

"We'll have to get you into the force, Braithwaite!"

The butler, fully aware of the superintendent's little jest, was nonetheless gratified. Oakes then asked for the phone so that he might call the "Flash and Dabs" crew, rather, as the men at the station called them, the Flask and Dabs crew. Since one man's name was Joe Black and the other's was Wilber White, they preferred that to being called the chess men.

Waiting for these two to come out from the station, Oakes returned to the little room and stood still again in the center of the room. Since Braithwaite had followed him, hoping to catch him in his curious new routine, Oakes held the man in a casual discussion of the staff and their habits, quirks, and customs. Oakes learned far more than the butler realized. This was why Oakes himself did so many of the interviews on his cases. People told you things even when they were not saying them. He approved of Braithwaite's fondness for Ann, and he approved of the butler's approval of her acceptance of her role as mistress of High Place Old Lodge. "For she had not been born to it, you know." He approved of Lady Anne's kindness to the staff and her genuine interest in them. Oakes reflected that this phenomenon might be explainable exactly because "she had not been born to it."

Also, there was the slight hint of the butler's approval of Lady Anne's letting the old man have pretty much his own say in High Place Old Lodge.

Around and around the superintendent went. Braithwaite started by trying to follow him but soon decided that it would be more dignified if he just stood to one side in a stable, less exhausting but still appropriately dignified position.

Then Oakes stopped going in circles.

"That photograph. Yes, that one there, just beginning to get the light from the window."

"Oh, I see, sir." Braithwaite was crushed. So that was all that it was! The light on a photograph! "Doubtless it should never have been hung there, sir. Not where the light could damage it so! I'll just have the footman take it down until we can arrange to have it hung in a more appropriate place."

"You'll leave it just right where it is until the Flash and Dabs men can do the job, if you don't mind! Meanwhile, you might tell me who all these men are. You needn't identify the birds in front of them or their firearms. I want names. Left to right, if you'll be so kind."

Bitterly disillusioned, but true to his calling, Braithwaite began at the left of the line of sepia gentlemen in their mustaches and plus fours, their guns and gun dogs, and named off all the gentleman as he came to them. Oakes nodded, seemingly as bored as the old butler was. When Braithwaite completed his assigned task, he turned to the superintendent.

"You've missed one."

"Begging your pardon, sir—?"

"The cocky little beggar there in the front, sitting down with the birds, the young one."

"Oh, you mean Percival Two, sir."

"What!"

"Well, we called him that, you see. Sort of a joke in the family. That was Richard Howard James Percival Riddecoombe, a cousin of, well, of our Percival. He was small, as you see. Small for his age, and the boys being boys, well, you know, they called him Dickie instead of Richard. Well, Dickie was what they called him when the adults were near. Boys being, as I said, boys. He would become furious! He idolized, well, our Percival, and he kept insisting 'I'm Percival too!' Meaning, of course, 'I'm Percival as well.' So the boys kept the joke going by calling him Percival Two. Just their little idea of a joke, as you might say."

"Boys being boys, as you say."

"Exactly so, sir. No harm in it, sir, not really!"

"No harm at all. No, of course not. They did look alike, did they? I mean as they reached the same ages?"

"Yes, sir. Well, the families were so very close. Too close, if you get my meaning, sir. Yes, they looked alike, and they were hellions alike. That is . . ." Here the old man stopped laughing and looked as if he were going to cry instead.

"Well, it was this way, superintendent. They both went for the army. Well, Sir Arthur, you know, he was a major, and the boys wanted to be serving their country as well."

"Like Sir Arthur." Oakes could not keep the bitterness out of his voice.

"Yes, well, I guess we're finding out a little different now. There was this night sortie, and young Percival Two led it, right into enemy territory it was, and he led it all right, only it was a trap, sir. Young Percival just had time to warn his mates, sir, and the whole thing blew sky-high. When the dust settled, there just wasn't anything left. Nothing to identify. Nothing to send home for his—his family. Just nothing."

Braithwaite came to a stop as if he had broken.

"They set up one of those monument things over at their place, but it was the end of the world for a while, it seemed like."

The silence went on for a long time.

"Percival Riddecoombe, shall we call him the first, came back all right, did he?"

"Oh yes. He came back. We got him back, all right."

Oakes was thinking hard, but he didn't want to disturb the old man. Knowing what they did know, what Scotland Yard knew now, and knowing the blackmailing going on even between the enemy lines, it did give the super something to think about. Yes, that was true for a fact.

Might Percival have walked right through and been beyond the enemies' lines before that bomb went off? Before all his chums were blown to bits? Further, say, two young men, each calling themselves Percival, really had come back? Who was to know? Arthur, of course, but who else? One Percival here, at a time at least, being Arthur's little brother. Doing his killing for him, and other odd jobs, of course. Meanwhile, the other one was giving the first one just the alibi he needed for the time. God, it didn't bear thinking about! That damn double image they kept getting of Percival in the skein! God, it *did* bear thinking about! But not here, not now.

Oakes shook himself as if to bring himself back to reality.

"You've had a great loss, Braithwaite. A great loss. Your have my sincere sympathy. Thank you very much for your help."

Oakes got out to the car as quickly as he could, growling at Black and White when they took their time over their equipment. He needed to think. He needed to share what he thought with Herrick and Ann. Soon.

"Here, White, you drive. I need to think, and this road's too damn . . . well, too damn something, anyway."

Black and White looked at each other and shrugged. Sometimes the higher-ups worked too hard, and that was a fact.

Chapter 36

The Reign Of Percival The First And Percival The Second

B ack at the station, Oakes took the dabs man aside. "White, you are free to think I've lost it."

"Thank you, sir." White, who didn't have to think overmuch in his aspect of the case, grinned. "I think you're just tired. This has all broken extremely quickly. We've all had to think around corners, I guess."

"You haven't heard what I want you to do yet."

"No, sir."

"Find the file of fingerprints for Percival Two."

"Sir?"

"There was another boy in the Riddecoombe clan about the same age as our Percy. He looked much like our Percy as well. He died, well, just say it this way. There was a war on. Richard Howard James Riddecoombe or something like that. Look it up, man!"

"Yes, sir, I remember." White was beginning to be seriously worried about the chief.

"It was hard to prove who had really died and who might have just walked off. If he had friends in high-enough places, he could have walked a long way off. Walked all the way home. Given the height of the friends and the situation at home. I'm thinking out loud here, and I know as well as you do that it sounds crazy. However, son, I outrank you, I think."

"Got that right, sir!"

"If I can find the prints of a dead boy anywhere on the files, I want you to look for them at High Place Old Lodge."

"But the time, sir! They won't have lasted. You know that, sir!"

"Except if my hunch is right—and there is some pretty good support here—I think they'll be fresh."

"But—"

"I think the boy is alive and well and giving us all kinds of grief. And I don't believe in ghosts."

Chapter 37

The Reign Of Herrick The First And Herrick The Second

The station house seen from the outside seemed to be a place where Oakes could think. He needed to think. He needed to stare at one of the copies of Ann's skein and try to fit his suspicions into it or find good hard factual reasons why they were the detritus of an overworked brain. Looks can be deceiving. Even, or especially, in police station houses.

"Sir."

Oakes knew he was in trouble—or had trouble. At any rate, he was not a man who was going to be given time to think.

"Yes, Sergeant. What is it this time?"

"Well, there's this lady, sir—"

"And she is where?"

"In your office, sir. I'm sorry, sir."

"You're just doing your job, son."

Son. He'd just called someone else son. Damn it, he was not getting old! Tired, yes, tired as hell, but he just needed rest! The station house had just lied to him. That was all.

He opened the door to the tiny room they had given him as an office. Hell, if they turned the room on its side and used one wall as the floor, there'd be more standing room.

"Yes, madam? What can I do for you? Is it something to do with this particular case? Because if one of the others can help you, I'd be grateful."

The woman stood up from the chair there was just room for by his desk. She was poised and polite as always, but he could tell panic was breaking out of that shell.

Oh god.

"I am Miss Makepeace from—"

"It's Charles, isn't it?"

I'm terribly afraid so, sir. He's been missing since last night. I called Missing Persons, but—"

"Right, they said it was too soon to worry, etc. Under the present circs, it is not too soon. You were very right to come to us." He motioned her to the chair again and sat down behind the desk. Evans opened his notebook.

"Please start from where he was going when he went missing. And does Allen know about this yet?"

"No."

"Good! Believe me, we'll work as hard as we can to find him before Allen finds out he's been missing. Now, please tell us all you know."

Charles had left a county meeting of real estate agents in Oakhill some thirty miles away at 10:00. He had not returned to his house and not returned to his office by opening time the next morning. By noon, when she had dealt with all she could at the office, she had come to the police, hoping to find the superintendent. She pointed out with deep concern," Since the younger Mr. Herrick is not presently with us, I am having to rely more and more on those young people in the front office." Her voice, always crisp and controlled, had wavered and whispered with uncertainty. Uncertainty was alien to Miss Makepeace, and Oakes, comparing her with the last times he had seen her, was struck as much by her change of appearance as by her words. Her eyes, usually so direct, were wavering back and forth as if trying to find Charles in the corners of the room. She was close to panic.

Doing as much as he could to reassure her, Oakes went immediately to the phone and began ordering a thorough search along the route that Miss Makepeace assured him that Charles "always, always took to these county meetings at Oakhill."

They were to look for a "large gray Buick suitable for an established real estate firm of excellent repute." She didn't know the year, but it was "very recent."

Oakes repeated her words over the phone, watching her closely as he did so.

He saw her long fingers in their gray gloves twist and untwist, rubbing the fabric mercilessly, straining at the seams. Her curling red-gray hair seemed to writhe away from helpless hairpins, creating the wild halo of some ancient Irish saint.

Miss Makepeace, consoled that all that could be done was being done, hurried back to Herrick, Makepeace, and Herrick in the hopeless hope that Charles had returned, but in reality to wait for a ransom note.

Oakes chose as his sergeant a clear-eyed youngster, a new man who had lived in the area all his life and knew every lane and trail that a large gray Buick could possibly have taken. Underhill was a break of luck for which Oakes gave fervent thanks. Slowly they traced the route. Oakes was watching one side of the road when Sergeant Underhill spotted weeds bent and broken on a deserted trail to a deserted farm on the other side. Living grass bends back when driven over, especially early in the year. Last year's weeds, taller than the new grass, were dried and brittle. They broke and stayed broken. Oakes and Underhill, with the other car behind them, drove up the silent track.

At the end, they found the ruin of a decaying farmhouse and an equally decaying barn behind it. Behind that, driven into the brambles and heavily scratched by the stout thorns not yet protected by sprouting young leaves, was a large gray Buick "suitable for an established real estate firm."

The police cars stopped some distance away from the car to let Oakes himself investigate so as not to interfere with any possible clues and to let Oakes find the body, if any.

There was no body. There was no blood. There was not even a sign of violence.

"Could he have gone willingly?" This from a young sergeant.

"Leaving those scratches on his impressive new Buick? Doubtful," Underhill replied from his deep understanding of the local lore and its inhabitants. "Very biddable was Mr. Charles, sir. Charming Charlie they called him at the Blue Boar. When it came to business, numbers and that, Miss Makepeace always had to be there. He'd have gone willingly just so they wouldn't put those scratches on his new car, would Charming Charlie."

Oakes felt he had just found the replacement for Constable Stites. Or rather more than a replacement for a constable. Why it hadn't happened years before was a mystery. Ann could have told him.

Flask and Dabs did their work, and the car was towed back to the station.

On the way back to High Yews, Oakes turned to Underhill.

"How do you read the case, Sergeant? I'd appreciate your views."

Every sergeant hopes to hear those words from his superior. Underhill was more than pleased to tell Oakes all he knew of the place and the people both. "Mr. Herrick? I mean Allen Herrick? How is he, sir?" Real concern showed in the young man's voice. "Begging your pardon, sir, but he's one of the good ones—the special ones, you know? He came back from the war so weary! So, like, scared inside himself. As if it wasn't over even yet, not for him. Now with him missing! I know the word is not to worry about him, sir, but, well, damn it, sir."

Oakes continued to be struck by this young man's concern and his perceptiveness. Oh yes! Promotion for sure. What were his superiors thinking? Where was the major in all this? Inquiries would be made.

"Finally, now, Sergeant, the one you've been avoiding. Mrs. Dray."

"Sir! Begging your pardon, she's none of us for all she's lived here forever. She's bad, sir, truly bad! I mean, it's like we don't even like to say her name, the way the oldens won't say, well, certain words, like the *little folk* or that. Superstition, sure, but still. Her and that Miss Tilly!"

Oakes nodded for him to go on. Underhill was holding his breath.

"Well, those two, they're both as mean as wildcats. Tilly, she don't amount to much. They think they can spread their mucky thoughts and nasty hints so secret, like, but we all know. Oh yes!" Underhill would have stopped there, given the chance. He was not given the chance.

"Go on!" Oh yes, young man, just keep going! Oakes was willing him to keep on talking. There was more he wanted out of this young man once he'd gotten him started.

Underhill, however, seemed to shy away. "Miss Tilly, now, Mrs. Dray has Miss Tilly like hypnotized as if she had some power over her."

Superintendent Oakes wanted to mention blackmail as that kind of power, but he didn't want to break into the young man's train of thought.

Underhill stopped there and stopped short. He was too close to his childhood fears. Oakes was happily convinced that he was not far short of the truth as well.

Now came the topic that had Oakes holding his breath. "Were there any others around, young children, for instance, who seemed to be interested in Mrs. Dray?"

Here it came—or didn't come.

"Well . . . There were two little boys, like twins they were, but just cousins, I reckon."

"Go on. Don't stop there!"

"Well, they were a little on the nasty side too, you know? Seeing as they were gentry, no one paid them much mind, not enough to stop them. Being as they were gentry, you know."

"Oh yes. I'll wager everyone said 'Boys will be boys.' Am I right?"

"Right, sir. You understand."

"And these boys had names?"

"That was the funny part of it."

"Go on, son! Don't just stop there!" Damned if Oakes was going to lead the young man, but this was taking all his control.

"Yes, sir. One was Percival, and the other was Percival as well. So they called the little one, the younger, they called him Percival Two."

Percival Two!

Some prayers were answered. With patience, some prayers were answered.

Chapter 38

The Dust Storm Again

A t last!

Oakes, in high good spirits, stopped by the office to drop off his finds from the gun room and to tell Sergeant White to go back and very politely ask to dust the picture of the hunting party. "For prints, you sap! Be a professional!"

White was thinking the super had lost his way in a big way, but he obeyed orders. It wasn't until he got back to the gun room and found that the picture was missing that he began to suspect maybe the super was deeper than he had thought. No amount of polite inquiry could explain the sudden disappearance of the faded picture of the gentlemen and their guns and their gun dogs. And their gun boy.

It was not in White's job description to press the issue, so he returned to the station pictureless, but with profound questions that he kept to himself lest the others think of him what he had so recently thought of the super.

When Oakes and Underhill got back in the car after collecting two more men who had made the mistake of having coffee in plain sight, Oakes gently announced that he had a warrant for the arrest for questioning of Mrs. Dorothy Alice Dray.

Mrs. Dray's house looked much like Mrs. Dray. She was destroying it as she had been in the process of destroying the Old Thatcher House—with a sort of vindictive carelessness.

The second car debauched its men, who disappeared around to the back of the house. Oakes went up to the front door and knocked with a vigor that just about had the thing off its hinges. No answer was received and none expected.

The two men in back had better luck. Oakes's abrupt appearance at the front had flushed their prey out the back. Mrs. Dray had made the mistake of trying to run.

"Trying to resist arrest, Mrs. Dray?" Oakes was heavily humorous. He was a happy man.

"Get out! You've no right! Laying hands on innocent people! I'll get you, you can bet on it! I'll get you, with my little friend."

"Now, now, Mrs. Dray." He smiled a smile that no one—no one—would ever trust. "I'm sure an innocent person like yourself will want to help the police in their continuing search for justice." He laid a hand, perhaps a clumsily heavy hand, on Mrs. Dray's right shoulder. She screamed and twisted away from him, spitting and growling.

"Still sore, Mrs. Dray? You need to have the doctor look at that for you. We only want to help. Now, we are all going to Dr. Coates's to see what he thinks. In case you're thinking of asking, yes, I do have a warrant for this, so you can help us with some questions we just can't understand. For instance, your little friend. The one who can be in two places at once?"

This was too much for Mrs. Dray. It took the two young men some time and some serious bruises to subdue her. Oakes cursed himself as hard as Mrs. Dray was doing. He had let his emotions get in the way of the execution of his duties. He could write himself up for this. The sooner they got her to Dr. Coates, the better!

Dr. Coates was out with a difficult birthing, but by luck Oakes didn't deserve, they found Nurse Appleby just coming in. Oakes briefed her on what she would find in the back of the car, and then cautiously they opened the back door and, with the nurse's help, got their "patient" into the office. This was the first time the superintendent had talked at any length with the nurse, and he was both surprised and more relieved than he hoped he showed. Superintendents are not as a rule happy to be surprised. She was sharp, perceptive, listened well, and heard probably more than he had intended. She supplied facts when requested and listened quietly when spoken to. A jewel without price. She was not at all surprised to find Oakes interested in Mrs. Dray. *About time too*, was her only thought.

Living in the heart of hunting country, Nurse Appleby was an expert in diagnosing shooting "accidents" and the lesser injuries involved in the sport—such as the deep bruise on Mrs. Dray's right shoulder.

"That's a shotgun bruise from a gun over the weight of the shooter and inexpertly used. Further, the wound was very inexpertly treated. About two or three days old, I'd say." Nurse Appleby stopped there.

Oakes nodded his agreement, satisfaction written all over his usually somber face. "God bless Nurse Appleby" was a phrase often heard in the country around High Yews.

"Dorothy Alice Dray, I am taking you into custody for questioning in the case of the murder of Sir Arthur Riddecoombe and the disappearance of Mr. Charles Herrick." On and on, the well-known warnings continued.

Dorothy Alice Dray, so warned, continued her mutterings as if they in themselves could protect her from the superintendent. Finally, another voice was heard, even more potent than that of Mrs. Dray's.

"Pull yourself together, woman. You are making a fool of yourself! Of all the ways to behave!"

Nurse Appleby, the good, the practical, the mother goddess of common sense, broke into the spell and smashed it into shards and fragments. Oakes shook his head like a stunned dog. Bless Nurse Appleby! Bless that woman!

He looked across at Underhill, wondering how he'd taken it. The boy had been badly shaken, but he was now more curious than anything. He leaned against the doorjamb with his head to one side, taking it all in. He'd do.

Dr. Coates, returning to what he expected to be his haven of sanity, came in just in time to give Mrs. Dray a veterinary-sized syringe of sedative and demanded to hear the whole story. He, as with Nurse Appleby, expressed no surprise, saying he had "seen it coming."

Why in blazes had no one done anything then! Oakes was amazed and furious, but this time he remembered his role in this drama and remained watchful and silent.

Dr. Coates was adamant that the woman needed medical supervision. Oakes agreed wholeheartedly. The thought of Mrs. Dray in one of the constable's jail cells was a horrific vision. Together, they made arrangements for both care and security at Wood's Edge. The important thing now was to get Allen and Ann to a safe house and Dray somewhere in high security, but for opposite reasons.

Together, Oakes and Allen planned for Ann's rescue and installation in a safe house.

Allen fought to stay out of the secure house. Things needed to be done, and he wanted to be the one doing them. Finally, as the reasons Oakes spelled out slowly and patiently for a man with little time and less patience soaked into Allen's head, he saw the logic and respected the mind behind Oakes's decisions. This was primarily Scotland Yard's case. Oakes had to keep his eye on too many pieces on the board as it was, one more too many with an extra Percival now in place.

Allen was not used to working in a subordinate role, but he quickly adjusted to Oakes's superior instructions and greater range of knowledge of the situation. Oakes, for his part, was quietly pleased with Allen's intelligence and experience. Those in a man willing to follow orders well, made a rare and useful man to have working with you. Respect for the other grew in both men as they finished up the detailed reports, the everlasting paperwork they both needed for their superiors.

At last Oakes was ready to call it a day when a young sergeant swung around the doorjamb.

"Officer, you will walk at all times as befits an officer of the law!"

"Sir! Yes, sir! But just listen!"

"Please stand at attention when addressing a senior officer, and believe me, son, I am a superior officer!"

"Yes! sir!" He saluted.

Allen came from the office around the corner.

"Aren't you at all curious, Superintendent? Sir?"

"And I'll have no cheek from you either, Mr. Civilian."

Oakes had definitely had a day too long by about twenty-four hours.

Allen, just a little overtired himself, entered into the rhythm of the thing. "If you don't ask him, I will. Sir."

"Against regulations, as you well know. Oh, all right! What is it that is going to keep us here another five hours?"

"Sir! French Security requests extradition of one Percival R. H. J. Riddecoombe—"

"Just the one?"

"Hush, this could be damn serious!"

"The gist of it is that they have one Percival, the above said Riddecoombe, and they rather think they are missing the other one of a set. They aren't more specific than that, but I rather think they have our Percival Two. However, it may be the other way around."

"Let me see that! Since arrest your side of person name of Major General Sir Grayson Hoving, they see their way clear on a number of issues and many arrests. They have—oh, come now! They have in their clutches one Percival S. D. T. R. de Valle, a.k.a. see list below, and are led to believe that we are withholding the other of the set. Would we please send the Percival Riddecoombe we are holding to them at our earliest convenience. With all due respect—"

"Thank you, Sergeant, that will be all!"

"Seriously, many thanks, by the way. Mustn't be grumpy over a gift like that!"

"I should say not! Now, how to lure P1 with bait consisting of P2?"

"Having a wonderful time, wish you were here?"
It's something to build upon."

"Come see what we found? Let's be good friends and share it? So many possibilities, aren't there?"

"This could almost be fun."

It had been a very long hard day.

And Oakes still hadn't told Allen about Charles going missing.

Chapter 39

Dark Of The Moon

After much of the cloak-and-dagger routine that Allen so despised, Ann and Allen were finally in the safe house, a small apartment that unfortunately had striped gray wallpaper so that it looked more like a cage than anything to soothe the nerves.

Oakes could see the stresses on the relationship as the situation changed but still failed to bring results. There were all the little differences that intimacy magnifies. Ann's strength that could so easily turn into obstinacy. Ann's kindness, her gentleness, on the other hand, could save them. Her sense of humor, usually gentle, could be the saving grace—God grant that it never turn bitter or biting.

Allen was much harder to read. For so many years under such pressure, might he have become a little inhuman himself? Sitting in this warm pseudo security, he seemed to expand and relax with his limbs loose and his smile ready and frequent.

Oakes worked to try to bring himself back to the cozy room, but too late.

"Bob, what? If there's good news and bad news, get the bad over with first."

Allen said simply, "Beer?" Allen knew what the bad news was going to be. What it had to be.

"Yes, thanks." The superintendent tried to smile, grateful for the short period of truce taken by the ritual of hospitality.

Settled again, he sipped his beer and began to say what had to be said. "Right," he said finally. "Here it is. Charles is missing. The evidence points to kidnapping. Points to kidnapping by Mrs. Dray. Mrs. Dray is under arrest and under observation in the most secure section of Wood's End.

"We have a very good case for murder one. Very good. The whole population is rejoicing. Except those of us who need to find Charles."

Oakes was getting all the bad news out as fast as he could. "We seem to have two Percivals. Allen will have told you a little about the business—some childish joke way back when Percival was in school. His cousin, a runt really named Richard but with a string of middle names including Percival, kept hounding our Percival and calling himself Percival too. They have found Percival Two alive in France and are trying to deal with him to get Percival One over there extradited on legit grounds for trial in France. That explains our problem getting a focus on our Percy in your skein, Ann. It could easily explain Mrs. Dray's mysterious 'little man' that she has had the countryside so spooked with."

Allen said, "Get it straight! You think Percival somehow has kidnapped Charles? Percival or Mrs. Dray? Which? Again, the motive—why? I mean, it would be easy enough to do, heaven knows. I spent enough times fishing him out of ponds and all that as a kid, but something here doesn't make sense, like a shark swimming in the kiddies' wading pool."

"It makes some kind of warped sense—if he and Dray are or were working together, and it is Dray who is using Charles to get something from you." Ann was looking at Allen with stark worry in her eyes.

"Does Dray—could she possibly know why you are here in High Yews? Aside from the fact that it is your home, I mean. Any professional reasons? Could there possibly be some connection with UQ? No." Oakes answered his own question.

"No. This is right here, right now! Dray and Percival!" Allen stood and started for the door, raging in frustration.

Oakes stood too, literally holding Allen away from the door. "Now do not get any idea of skipping out and taking it upon yourself to go for him. You've got all of Scotland Yard after your brother right now. Allen! Damn it! Ann—make him listen!" Oakes's frustration was filling the room like an electrical storm.

"Think! Allen, think! Where could anyone hide Charles? Who would know where to take him?"

Allen was white with fury. He turned on Oakes. "How long have you known Charles was missing? I agreed to play this your way, damn it!"

Ann took Allen's arm. "Allen, if Charles is not with Mrs. Dray, then the whole witchcraft hold over the community aspect of Mrs. Dray is not there. If Charles is hidden and Percival is going to send a lovely, polite—or a crude, nasty—little ransom note, then the chances are that he has hidden Charles in some dusty attic at High Hill Old Lodge. I assume you've spent some time with Miss Tilly? She is the housekeeper and, in theory, should know the house."

Ann glanced at the superintendent. "You've met her, Bob?"

A definite nod of the head and a definite shudder. "Yes, she takes people that way."

"Both of you sit down and listen to me! What you are both forgetting is that I was mistress of High Place Old Lodge. The lodge is not old, and while many of the staff are old, they did not grow old together! I have lived at the lodge as long as Miss Tilly, and I know far more about it, about the hidden cupboards and secret stairs and all the places where people hide—have hidden in the past. A short piece of history of the lodge that would come in useful to you now is that the house was built for a very unpleasant mother-in-law who terrorized the young couple up at High Place. She was deprived of that pleasure by being sent to the dower house. High Place Old Lodge was the name Arthur gave it when he bought it—a very recent name. After she was sent there, in relative solitude—incidentally, that is why the house itself is in such relative solitude away from the rest of the estate—the servants, out of self-defense, found their way into the secret ways of getting from one room to another without being seen. The servants were the ones who found places around and above the servant quarters where they could go without being found. The children followed the paths that the servants found. Don't go to Miss Tilly for your questions about High Place Old Lodge. Come to me."

Ann spoke quietly but with such authority that both men stared. That was the voice of the widowed Lady Anne Riddecoombe, her dignity, her command of respect. Oakes later forgot this, to his peril. "When we are let out of kennel, I can show you the places above the attics that have been boarded up and the holes in the foundation where the brandy was hidden. All of these are places that could have been used by Mrs. Dray with or without the help of poor Miss Tilly. Have you thought that however Miss Tilly might be afraid of you, Superintendent, she is even more terrified of Mrs. Dray?"

Oakes was having trouble adjusting to this new Lady Anne/Ann. Evidently, Allen was having similar problems.

"Ann, my love, are you still in there?"

She flashed him a smile so full of tenderness and love his eyes closed for a moment, and he felt for her hand.

Oakes got up and looked down at the two of them. Both powerful people. Both extremely intelligent. Just how long could he expect to be able to keep them "in kennel" as Ann—as Lady Riddecoombe—had put it.

"Lady Riddecoombe, if we don't have a startling success soon, may I take you up on that?"

"Of course, Superintendent. I might just say that it is just a trifle too damn late for you to be starting out on this?"

"Damn." He had come in as "Bob" and he was going out as "Superintendent." Good job, sir. Well done, that man!

Allen had gone to the door to let Oakes out—or to be sure that he went. This courtesy was to net him some information the superintendent would rather Allen had gone without. The very young detective on duty had just received some information to give the super. So full of his own importance and so empty of caution, he blurted it out without thinking, without looking who might be with the superintendent.

Oakes took the young sergeant off for a quick and forceful lesson in holding one's tongue on duty, but not before Allen heard the first excited few words—all the words he needed to hear, really.

"It's that Mrs. Dray, sir. They say she's escaped!"

Chapter 40

Dangerous Storm Brewing

P ercival had Charles, and Mrs. Dray was loose.

"Dear God," Allen prayed, "let me get to Charles before she does!" Carefully and with great deliberation, he locked all the locks and set all the bolts. Then, equally carefully and with equal deliberation, he rested his head on the doorjamb and tried to think.

When Allen did not come back to the sitting room, Ann came to him. She walked quietly with just enough whisper to her skirts to let him know she was there. "Allen?"

Allen turned and, groaning, brought her into his arms.

"Oh, Ann! Damn it all!"

Ann nestled into his shoulder, holding him tightly. Then she leaned back a little and looked into his eyes.

"Since you are going to go, you had best know all you can about the holes of High Place Old Lodge. Since I am your most reliable source, we'd better talk before you go, hadn't we?"

Ann turned and led him back to the sofa. Allen stared for a second before he followed. Oh yes, Ann could still surprise.

Allen listened intently, his eyes focused on the bare top of the coffee table where the beer had been a short time ago. Ann went over High Place Old Lodge level by level, cellars to attics. All the out-of-the-way places where boys like Percival—either Percival—would play and hide. Hiding was such an important part of playing for some, a trait some never quite grew out of and would never quite forget.

Ann smiled, or tried to. Allen honored the attempt.

"Please remember Mrs. Dray. You've gotten an impression of Mrs. Dray, but I warn you, whatever you think, if she escapes, she will be worse."

"*If* she escapes!" So Ann hadn't heard. Thank God for that!

"If she escapes"—strangely, she echoed his thought—"don't misjudge her for her pride and her stupidity. Her cunning is the cunning of a trapped ferret. She has no friends, but many live under her influence. She uses threats, very believable, powerful threats. She knows what these people fear, and she uses it. If she threatens, she carries it out. She has no compunction about killing a cow or burning a barn. Kidnapping a brother, especially one as, well, as naive as Charles can be, would be like going berry picking.

"Miss Tilly has collapsed and will not recover until Mrs. Dray is scotched, if then.
Constable Stites is another."

"Stites!"

"Of course! Allen Herrick, think! Why does no one report the dead cow or the ruined barn?"

"Ann, when I've gone. After I leave, call Oakes and tell him all you know about Stites. This goes way back in time, doesn't it? Another layer in your skein. Write! Ann, write again now! Then call Oakes. If he's not in his office, tell them to find him! He needs to know all of this ASAP."

Allen led Ann to the table they had set up for her writing, and Allen made sure she got started. Then, always quietly, he wandered off into the kitchen.

Ann wrote. She found there was something to write about. Threads of power, of fear, and of anger. Motives. She wrote and thought and wrote again. The apartment grew quiet—the quietness that came over it when the quietness of Allen was gone.

Ann went through the apartment, just to make sure. Then she went to the phone and got Oakes. Oakes, still wide-awake, listened intently to Ann's story, her skein. He asked her to go slowly about it and took notes as she went.

Ann stopped while Oakes shouted orders. Then she continued with each connection, each strand of influence, each line of power, all through the skein. Ann told Oakes all she had told Allen about Mrs. Dray and High Place Old Lodge.

Finally she said, "He's gone, you know. Allen's gone."

Chapter 41

The Calm Before The Storm

"**C**ould you ring up the vicarage? I'd like Mrs. Matthews to help me keep watch." She hung up the phone.

Then Ann wept. Silently, she took out her latest version of the original skein and tried to concentrate on weaving the new threads into the old patterns. She was still trying and still weeping when Amity knocked on the door.

"Amity! Oh, thank God! If you love me, help! Help me think! I need yarn for my skein! And comfort for my sanity!"

"Anything, Ann, my love. You know that—anything! Could you just bring me up to date a bit? I know Allen's gone off to find Charles on his own, which is possibly foolish, but quite understandable, don't you think? Now, what, my dear? How can I help you?" Amity had led Ann over to the sofa and was stroking her hand.

Ann took a deep breath. "Do you know about the skein?"

"Not really, dear." Amity's eyes were concerned. "I'd like to know more, of course, but not anything that would put anyone in danger, of course. I mean, I gather that I'm being trusted somewhat or I wouldn't be here. I also do realize that you're in danger or *you* wouldn't be here. So please, Ann, tell me what is safe for me to know. I do so want to help!"

Amity always smiled, but she had a way of smiling particularly when she meant to aim that smile straight into your soul. Ann smiled back gratefully.

"What I desperately need is for you to tell me—to tell me all about the people here, as you know them now and knew them before the war."

"Surely, my love." Amity was not the giver out of automatic love. If Amity said *love*, she meant love. It was not her middle name. It was her first name. It was her soul.

"I want you to tell me all you can about Stites and Mrs. Dray."

"Oh! Surely they know? Quickly then. There were three Stites brothers. Tom, the oldest, went to London and made something of himself. He went into the war as an officer and died in Normandy. Rich, the middle boy, was the constable here for a long time, and a good one. When Tom was killed, Rich fought to be enlisted, even though he held a necessary homeland position. After a long fight, they enlisted him. That left the last brother . . . something of a runt, I'm afraid. He would never have become constable without the wonderful records of the two older brothers. He never should have become constable, and in a way, he never did. I don't know when we realized quite how much he was under the influence of Dot Dray."

"So the—I cannot keep calling people the locals. That is very much too High Place Old Lodge. Amity, what do you call the people here?"

"We. Us. Those of us who live here. Simply us."

"Right. That makes me one of the others. Always one alone. One of them, never one of us." Ann's fear was getting the better of her. Her tears came again. Fear, fatigue, and helplessness so long held back threatened to swamp her, drown her, drag her down to—

"Ann! Come here this minute! You are one of us! Stop this! Take that step towards us. Take me through the skein!"

Ann shook her head as if she had lost all her strength in deep water. She stared at her friend. "Friend?" Ann had not realized that she had said the word aloud.

"Of course, friend!" Amity grabbed Ann's hand. "Of course! Feel that! Trust that! Now! The skein! What do you think that I know that you don't know? Something that would fit into your skein? Is the skein on paper or only in your head? Show me! Tell me! Now!"

Ann showed her the new skein and the skein of the past. "It's only based on what I can see now, and that is sheer ignorance, of course."

Amity studied the complex of names and connecting lines. Lines leading to and lines leading from. Lines that stopped in knots. Amity's respect for Ann grew. Allen had talked of Ann, of course. Talked proudly. Amity had no idea, no idea at all, of this—this multidimensional dynamic structure of past, present, them, us, lines of power, of fear, over time, from them over us, from us over them, each affecting, changing themselves and the lines they touched, knotted themselves into each other. Lines from the past changing the lines continuing into the future. The shadow lines. The ones that no one saw should be there but were, and so no one saw what they did to the other lines. The "lower classes," the "local people," having such power over the "upper classes," the "country against the "county."

Not to be thought of! Never to be thought of! Sir Arthur having power over Dot Dray? Of course, the whole parish knew about that, about Sir Arthur having Dot's car towed off his property and to the dump. Dot Dray having power over Sir Arthur? Dot Dray killing Sir Arthur with his own shotgun? Dot Dray killing Sir Arthur *because* he had such power over her. Had used that power so cruelly, so humiliatingly!

Finally, Amity raised her eyes to Ann's. They had wells of awe in them. Awe and a puzzled loss of balance. Surprise, yes, but fear as well.

"Dear Lord! You've seen us near naked. Boy and man, man and master, and all these lines! Strands. Colors. Fear! Anger! Revenge! Is this how you see us, Ann?"

"I'm looking for a murderer, Amity. I'm looking for a person who may, quite easily, kill Charles. Kill Allen! Tonight, Amity! Of course there are lines of love, of respect, of pleasure and pride in each other. Those lines don't kill. These do!"

Amity tried to think of the lines between herself and Ann and failed. Had she failed?

No! She had not failed. She herself, Amity Matthews, had created the line—the strong line from herself to Ann. It was a line of love, of comfort, of support. That line was there because she had made it be so. The eyes she had for a moment feared she now saw were smiling at her.

"Oh, my love, give me a minute!" Amity drew in a deep breath. "I had no idea! I can see now why you are so afraid. The lines from Dot Dray—well, to everyone—are so very dark! You think they—Allen, Charles, Dot Dray—are in the same place right now? The lines meet there, don't they?"

"Yes. They meet. Think for a minute what that could mean, Amity! I know that Allen has had much more training in this sort of thing than Dot Dray ever imagined. I also know that Dot Dray has no honor, no compunction, no compassion, none of the things I love Allen for. So each has one advantage. Oh, Amity, I am afraid. Dot has escaped, you know. One of the sergeants was telling Superintendent Oakes as he left here. So, yes, by now, I imagine they are very close to the same spot in the heart of the skein.

"Dot Dray is missing, Charles is missing, Allen is missing. As if to make up for all that, we now have two men called Percival."

"Oh, my love, don't look at me like that. They told me not to tell you. You have told me, haven't you? With your skein."

"Yes. Superintendent Oakes decided to be 'them' instead of us. So he couldn't see all the lines. That's why I had to show the skein to you, Amity. You could see the lines, couldn't you? See what they meant?"

"How close we each are to each other, for good or for ill. Yes, Ann, I see."

The doorbell rang. Ann recognized Superintendent Robert Oakes and silently let him in. Oakes tried to smile. It was a failure, and he knew it. He glanced hesitantly at Mrs. Matthews. Ann remained silent.

"How much have you told her?"

"Which one of us are you asking?"

"Ann, please, listen. We have not found Allen. We have not found Charles. We have not found Mrs. Dray. We've wasted all our shot. You'll be as safe as Scotland Yard can make you, believe me."

"As safe as Allen? As safe as Charles?"

Amity cried out. Never had she heard Ann so bitter.

"We need you, Ann. We need you 'out of kennel,' as you said at one point." He did smile that time. "We are almost positive that they are all in High Place Old Lodge. We've spent about twenty-four hours searching the place. We've torn down walls and chipped out brick."

Slowly, Ann walked around the room, possibly looking for everything she might need. It seemed to Amity that Ann was looking around the room to memorize it, as if she were seeing it for the last time. Ann finally turned to smile at Amity, gave the latest copy of the skein to Oakes, and walked out the door and down to the waiting police car.

Amity had closed her eyes. Left alone in the small room with its striped wallpaper, Amity was praying.

Chapter 42

The Heart Of The Skein

A llen was in a space much smaller than the small room he had left some hours earlier. It needed no striped wallpaper to resemble a prison cell. This room, this space—even that word was more than it deserved—was darker, infinitely more dusty, musty, and sickeningly moldy. Mrs. Dray, in the dim glow of a small oil lamp, seemed to have grown in size and power, as if photosynthesis had found its opposite. Her dark clothes, shapeless in the gloom, seemed to shade into the dark behind her so she continuously encompassed them all.

Her breathing in the cramped space rasped loudly until it seemed the only breathing.

Her eyes reflecting the dim light of the little oil lamp seemed more brilliant than the lamp itself. They flickered as she gazed in triumph from one dim face to another. Her mouth, open with the effort to drag in the airless air, was the image found in medieval manuscripts of the living mouth of hell itself. The closeness of the air in the windowless cavity made the air when it was breathed seem what it was—already used up, already sucked empty of whatever life-giving power it might have once had.

Charles's sudden sneeze seemed the worst of some already-disgusting black comedy. Everyone held their own breath as long as they could to avoid bringing into their own lungs the sickening moisture. Until they realized that that moisture was already what they were holding in.

Allen's first thought was of the misery his asthmatic brother must be suffering. His upper lip glistened with what was only partly sweat. With his hands bound in front of him, he could only gasp and gulp and try ineffectively to wipe his nose on his once-immaculate jacket sleeve. How long could he last in this room?

"How long does it take a dimwit like you to climb a simple ladder?" Mrs. Dray shouted to Percival, who had just finished reading the note Allen had slipped to him. Allen had convinced Percival that he had just smuggled it out of Oakes's office to bargain with. It had Hoving's name on it.

"I can't climb the damn thing one-handed now, can I?" Percival tried for a sneer and failed. He set his torch down so that it illuminated the highest rungs of the makeshift ladder. Not even a moth could live to flutter around its dim light. Percival stayed close to the trap door, partly because there was no place to move farther into the cramped space, and partly—Allen had to hope—because he was already planning to leave as quickly as he could and still make it out alive.

"Be greedy!" Allen wished him. "Want more! What is here for you? France is out there in the sunlight! In the air! Go to France!"

Charles sneezed again, gagging this time.

"To hell with this!" Percival shouted suddenly. "I'm for better things than this! God, you'll all rot! You're rotting already." He glared at Charles and suddenly disappeared down the ladder, leaving the small space darker as the light of his torch grew dimmer and disappeared.

There was a bare moment of silence before Mrs. Dray bawled after him, "Be here no more! Go! I need you no more! Do you hear me? I'm free!"

Free but completely out of breath. Percy could still be heard in the distance scuffing up the ubiquitous dust that only made him cough more.

"Mrs. Dray, let Charles go before you kill him. Let him carry your ransom note to Lady Anne. No one will pay for his body. Lady Anne will ransom me using the late Sir Arthur's money. Fitting, don't you think?" Allen tried to smile slyly but failed. Mrs. Dray didn't notice. What she was watching was in her own head. Her smile was ophidian.

Charles was gagging and gasping and turning green in the dim light. Mrs. Dray cut his hands free and pushed him roughly down the ladder.

"I want 100,000 pounds by tomorrow night" she bellowed. "By tomorrow night or she doesn't see lover boy alive again!"

Allen was chilled to the bone. There was not the slightest doubt that she meant it.

She was gasping and coughing herself now or her demands would have been more elaborately lewd and specific.

Percival had escaped. Charles was escaping. Allen could hear him catching his breath and stumbling toward the only minuscule window on the floor below. Allen could have shouted with relief as he heard the glass in the small window break. That meant air! Air for Charles. As long as Percy had kept going and not waited with that revolver, Charles would be safe!

Now for Mrs. Dray.

The smothering pressure of her weight was missing from his back. Where was she going? Where could she go? Allen had scanned the airtight space when he first was shoved up the ladder. As his eyes adjusted, he kept scanning, but it was all just shades of gray shading into further shades of gray. Farther shades of gray? Gray farther away? Yes! She thought she could escape through the tiny space behind her. She had tried to escape through the tiny space behind her. The mansion on the hill where she and the boys, Percival One and Two, had grown up had towers lifting high over the roof. This child's version of the mansion had towers as well, but they were a child's image of castle towers. More importantly, they were child-sized castle towers.

Mrs. Dray was by no stretch of the imagination the young woman she had been when she had chased the boys through those towers and escaped through those bolt-holes. She had grown and the tower had changed, so that instead of snaking through the narrow space, she stuck like a bung in a barrel. She couldn't go forward, and she couldn't go back. Splinters in the rough wood pinned her in whatever she did. She could see freedom through the narrow escape hole, but that did her no good. She couldn't escape to it.

"Your 'little man' has gone before you, Dorothy." True enough. Allen was merely stating the unalterable fact. Mrs. Dray—the self-indulgent, overweight adult Mrs. Dray—was no longer the young Dorothy. This tower was not the castle tower she had slithered through with such ease before to catch her "little man." It no longer mattered which little man, which Percival it was anymore. Her determination changed to panic. She had wedged herself between the rough floor and the rough walls that held up the slates that sloped down to the floor on all sides. She had trapped herself. She continued to trap herself.

Chapter 43

Dusty Déjà Vu

"What exactly are we looking for?"

"I am looking for dust. You are here to protect me while I look for dust."

"But there is dust everywhere!" Oakes was a tired and a very frustrated man.

"Superintendent, the dust is like the tall grass in a field. You can see where people have been and where they were going. There are trails and paths in the dust, some earlier and some later, overlapping. We are looking for those trails. It is like a map of footprints or of where things have been kicked or dragged. It's all there."

She seemed to think it hardly worth explaining. There it all was, right in front of him. There was the trail, some of it still hanging in the air, of Percival's escape.

"Someone obviously came or went along that trail of dust. Can you see it?" She meant "Can't you see it?

The super knew it. Now that she showed him, yes, of course he could see it. He sent two men off to follow that trail while it was still fresh—if you could call dust fresh.

The crash of breaking glass above their heads was a sharp, startling violation of the silence. They ran to the next level and could see Charles slumped by the tiny window. He was breathing. Long deep breaths with a cough at each exhale.

Sometimes the coughs took over, and he had to will the breaths to start again.

"Get him down to the ambulance ASAP," Oakes ordered, urgency plain in his voice. One of the men picked up Charles's right shoe and gently shook the glass out of it before he slipped it back on Charles's right foot. They moved off in the gray gloom. Slowly, but always toward the light.

Oakes, Ann, Underhill, and two more kept going along the now-obvious path Charles had taken to the window.

"Hello? Ann, is that you? With Oakes, I gather. Shut up, Mrs. Dray. You've lost. Closet, Ann. Think closet. Think déjà vu."

Déjà vu indeed! Ann's back crawled, and she had to breathe deeply. Wisely, she went over to the window to do this.

With great care, Oakes managed the shallow rungs. He stopped a few rungs short of the top and took in the shadowy scene.

"Good evening, Mr. Herrick."

"Is it? Then good evening, sir. May I say how good it is to see you, however dimly."

"Ann is here, as you might guess. Is there anything you would care to shout to her?" Then "Good Lord! How did you get her to do that?"

It was obvious to all that the superintendent did not mean Ann, although one or two of the newer recruits glanced nervously at her.

As more torches were brought up and placed around the narrow space, Oakes could see a pair of tiny woman's shoes, still kicking.

"Mrs. Dray has gotten herself in a bind, sir. She is pinned down in her position, sorry, sir, by a nasty collar of splinters. We'll need help with this one. Careful as you go, sir. She can still kick like a mule."

"I've sent a man to look for rope in the gardener's shed. Though tape from a bathroom might work well. Harder to get off, maybe." There was a kind of happy anticipation in his voice.

"Unfortunately, the dust will make it harder to stick tight."

"Careful now. Those splinters won't give up easily. We'll have to pull her out against the grain."

Suddenly, Mrs. Dray's head came free of its yoke. The mutters became yowls and curses. Kicks thudded against the floor and against flesh.

"I did warn you, Super. Did she break anything?"

"Is Coates there yet?" Oakes shouted down the ladder. "Mrs. Dray seems a trifle overwrought and a possible danger to herself and others. I'll come down first. 'Ware feet below!" The superintendent avoided the ladder entirely and simply jumped to the lower floor.

"OK, Doctor, seems we'll be bringing the patient to you instead. Richards, you and who's left down there? Jack, you be ready to receive. This is just going to be awkward as Hades, my lads. She's worn herself out, but it won't be forever. If she wakes up halfway down, it'll be hell to pay. We've got a rope under her arms, and we'll

198

lower her as slowly and easy as we can, but that's a fond hope. Ready? Here goes!"

A pair of heavily roped and taped legs appeared over the edge of the trapdoor.

"Damn! How'll we do this, Herrick? Right. OK, lads, we'll have to cut some rope so her knees'll bend. Worse off for you if she wakes up in transit. Now feet, now legs. OK, lads, she's sitting on the edge. We'll launch her as slowly as we can. You be ready to take the weight. Remember, it'll be dead weight, as it were."

Oakes was halfway into a warning when the rung bearing her weight broke, and she came down upon them.

Gasping, they dragged her into the attic room and over to the window. Dr. Coates, with a mask from his black bag over his mouth, knelt down by Mrs. Dray with a hypodermic needle in his hand.

Allen lowered himself onto the broad shoulders of a young constable and climbed down gratefully to the attic room floor. Dr. Coates, looking up from Mrs. Dray, saw blood and came quickly to Allen's side as he leaned carefully out the window, trying to avoid the broken glass surrounding it.

"All right, young man, where does it hurt?"

Allen started to laugh and then thought better of it. He turned as Dr. Coates stripped off his jacket and his shirt. Ann's eyes took him in as if she could heal his pain with her love. By the window, her face lit by the gray light lit up the shining streaks diagonally across her cheeks where her tears had run.

"Oh, Allen, my love," she choked, laughing and crying. "What a dustup."

Chapter 44

Calm After The Storm

The survivors were all in positions of varying but complete relaxation in Ann's comfortable but still anonymous home. Ann and Allen had found their usual places on the sofa they had found together at the last estate sale. Superintendent Oakes was truly ensconced in the huge old chair by the fireplace. Amity was on the smaller chair on the other side of the fireplace. Letty and Gil were, as always, together, this time on the chairs by the writing table. They looked like puppets content to have their strings cut.

It was early evening, and the first cool breezes came in with the low sun through the broad bay windows. Early evening birds murmured outside. No one wanted to break the exhausted peace. The comfortable peace. The contented, safe, peace.

It was hard to believe that Mrs. Dray had lost her power. Hard to realize what a wide range of power she had over the community she had controlled for so many years, all the way from maid to master. Unbelievable. Undeniable.

Ann's skein had become a work of art and a web. A web with no holes through which an ego as large as Mrs. Dray's could escape. Mrs. Dray had been counting on weaknesses like her own—weaknesses she could understand and use. The Allen she had seen had not existed. She had assumed weaknesses that were not there but that had trapped far more sophisticated, experienced, and greedy blackmailers before Mrs. Dray.

Allen had just concluded much of the same story he had earlier told in giving evidence at the Yard. Oakes had followed him closely this time as well. He had not strode back and forth, jingling his keys this time, but nevertheless had followed every word and still asked questions that took the story off at different angles, showing new aspects of what they knew. When this happened, Oakes would mutter, pick up his pencil, and add a new line or two to the notebook, the one that had been new a week or so ago. Now Oakes had come to its last few pages.

The case was far from over. Paperwork far more extensive and daunting than the brief lines he had jotted in his notebook loomed ahead. The dangers were over though. Thank God they were really over now. No good people lost. Two exceptionally good people had been found.

Allen Herrick had left UQ and had been offered a responsible position at the Yard. He had mentioned the need to talk with Ann about it first. Scotland Yard—the AC—had strongly suggested that Oakes use his influence there, unofficially of course.

One higher-up had joked about the need to get Ann if they could not get Allen. *A. Herrick* at the bottom of a page could be sufficiently ambiguous to pass. This would come back to haunt said higher-up.

Van Eyck broke in to the blessed quiet with an expressed dissatisfaction with the side of the door she was on. Gil got up slowly and let her in, checking for possible presents that would be better not presented to her mistress.

Amity left first, hugging Ann warmly and then hugging Letty. That friendship would grow as well.

Oakes got up and went to the door, trying to ask Allen questions without actually coming out and asking them. Surely real estate would be awfully boring after all this? Oakes went to the car and waited for Allen.

Gil and Letty wandered out to the orchard, causing Van Eyck to reverse her preference on sides of doors.

Then Allen leaned gingerly on the doorjamb, pulling Ann toward him. Ann very gently pulled back. Allen made no objection. He cherished her warmth.

"Oh, Allen, my own dearest love, I could swat you so hard!"

"Not the proper tone, surely, my most precious one." Then his voice lost its joking lilt. Then lost any sound at all.

Minutes passed. A police car sounded its horn. It was ignored.

Finally they drew apart.

"Ann, I've been offered a position, a very good one, at the Yard."

"Yes?"

"I've told them I'd have to talk with you first."

"Yes?"

"Well?"

"Yes. Yes. And yes!"

More silence.

"Would it be too much to ask for a desk job?"

Allen's laughter sounded loud and clear out the open door and then was curiously muffled again.

Oakes turned off the engine and leaned back. Then Allen's steps were heard through the grass, strong, striding, coming to the car. Coming to the future.

Epilogue

Percival At Sea

I t had been a peaceful crossing, proving that the sun can shine on the English Channel. On the French side, anyway. This time was especially special Percival thought because it meant never having to do what Arthur demanded ever again. The Channel breeze ruffled his hair. All right. The Channel wind blew through his hair. Wind was much more exciting than a breeze anyway. Wind pushed things. It could make things move. It could make things happen. The way he would make things happen in France. Now that Arthur was not there to make things happen his way, he, Percival, would make them happen his way! Yes! Now that Arthur was gone, he, Percival the First, would do all the thinking and the doing—all of it! He had never been able to think while Arthur was alive. Never.

Good old Mrs. Dray! Percival laughed at the thought! Now he could tell little Percy Two what to do. As it should be. Percival One would plan and do and make all that money now! In France. France was lovely! Sunshine, wine, fast cars! With Percy Two to push around! It was only justice! All his life, Arthur had pushed Percival, the real one, around. Well, that would stop now, wouldn't it? Imagine that little twerp actually writing him. Telling him all about the new setup in France. Beautiful France! Imagine putting it all in paper there where the cops could read it! Smart, not!

He could see Percy Two waiting for him! The silly twit! To welcome him. To welcome him to walk right in and take over. The whole setup . . . Wait a minute. There was Percy Two, smiling and waving, but who were the other two, one on each side of Percy Two? Lots bigger than Percy Two. What did they have to do with Percival the Free in beautiful France? They didn't look like they were going to be any fun. Or have things all ready for the new regime. Regime, that was a good word. It meant he would rule, do what he pleased. He liked the sound of it—regime.

Who were these two on either side of him here on the boat? These two were in his way. He couldn't see France through these clowns, could he? Extra what?

Handcuffs? In France? He'd never liked France anyway. Oh, they would let him come home after the trials, would they? For more trials? Hey, you can't do that, can you? Percy, you little twit, what sort of game are you playing? Invite me to France, would you? He knew about Napoleonic Law. No, it wouldn't work that way for him! Percival the Smart knew a thing or two. You can't try a man twice for the same offense! That was it! More than enough offense to go around? For him and Percy the Twit as well?

No, not going to happen. Papers? What papers? Oh, those papers. Well, forgeries, weren't they. Oh, yes, every one. Hid them there just to trip you up! Knew it all the time!

Yes, definitely. Oh, he could prove it all right! Yes, he had friends. In England and France, of course, you twit! What did they mean "already in custody"? But the law is only there to be gotten around!

Honest!

An introduction to the next book of the Skein:

SECRETS OF THE SKEIN

Ann Herrick is a survivor. To be able to survive she invents, or discovers, or recovers? the Skein. The very source of the Skein is a mystery—an ancient mystery. As she studies it, she grows with it until she becomes an expert in its ability to see in many dimensions the emotions, love, hate, greed, envy, compassion, and trust—or lack of it—as bright and dark strands connecting people and giving Ann images to help Scotland Yard understand the dynamics, and the motives they need to solve the crimes they must investigate. Her husband is also a survivor, a British secret agent in World War II, recovering from his injuries to become an agent for Scotland Yard, using his war experience, his cool daring, and his remarkable intelligence in combating postwar crime. The bond between Ann and Allen is based not just on the love they find as they work together, but also on a depth of trust and loyalty few can discover. Their new friends seem to have developed the special skills of survivors as well—bringing their own unique talents to the understanding of the Skein. One new-found friend is handsome, clever Stephano, former undercover agent for the Allies in his native Italy, silently bearing old wounds, but now looking to a bright future as a respected expert in the art treasures he worked so hard to recover and restore to their rightful owners, after the terror and the chaos of war. Another survivor, yet to discover her full powers, is quiet Elaine who must overcome a bitter past of treachery and betrayal to uncover the mysteries in a Renaissance book of ancient knowledge, which she finds hidden during her research on the histories of the works of art Stephano is still recovering. These friends, new and old, create a bond of loyalty and friendship they must trust completely as they battle an almost invisible power of darkness that only they can see as they follow the strands of the Skein.

About the Author

Elizabeth Schaeffer has written in several different formats, from professional papers on medieval art to newspaper columns on wildflowers. Her master's thesis was accepted into the Medieval Arts Collection of the J. P. Morgan Library, and she is the author of the previously published book Dandelion, Pokeweed, and Goosefoot. She currently lives in New Hampshire.

CPSIA information can be obtained at www.ICGtesting.com
Printed in the USA
LVOW13*0838240614

391436LV00008B/46/P

9 781466 933118